After the Raid

REBECCA BRIDGES

Printed and Bound in the United States of America

This book is an original publication of Outboard Publishing LLC

Interior design: Rebecca Bridges Outboard Publishing LLC
Cover design: Jim Eberwein COT Publishing
Photos:
 FreeImages.com/Flavio Takemoto Binary Code 2
 FreeImages.com/Gavin Spencer Beach Romance
 FreeImages/Sanja Gjenero Lonely Couple

First printing August 2018

ISBN 978-0-9975718-4-4

This is a work of fiction. References to events, establishments, organizations or locales are intended only to provide a sense of authenticity, and are used fictitiously. The only name of an actual person is Lucinda Edwards. Lucinda's actual job title and fact she is a U.S. Army veteran are the only true facts, all other incidents, background and dialogue are drawn from the author's imagination and are not to be construed as real. All other names, characters, incidents and dialogue, are drawn from the author's imagination. Any resemblance to actual persons, living or dead, or actual events is purely coincidental.

AFTER THE RAID

DEDICATION

I dedicate this novel to Lucinda Edwards, the inspiration for this book. In real life she is indeed a computer security specialist with the Department of the Army as well as a U.S. Army veteran. All other incidents, background and dialogue contained within this book are drawn from the author's imagination and are not to be construed as real. Any resemblance to actual events is purely coincidental.

TITLES BY REBECCA BRIDGES

After the Reunion: Sons of Magnolia Meyers Series, Book One

Blue Ridge Mountain Escape

CONTENTS

CONTENTS

ACKNOWLEDGMENTS

A special thank you to Mike Aldridge, retired DEA agent and Betty Houbin. Mike graciously shared his knowledge of DEA procedures with me. Betty is an advocate for human trafficking victims and provided me an insight into this horrible activity. If there are any mistakes in this book about the DEA or human trafficking they are mine alone due to a misunderstanding.

Once again a big thank you to all the members of the Coastal Authors Network and Carolina Forest Authors Club. Your support, enthusiasm and critiques helped me complete this manuscript.

Saving the best for last, thank you Betty Bolte, editor extraordinaire. This book is better for having your expert eye review it. I look forward to our next collaboration.

CHAPTER ONE

Lucinda Edwards hunkered down at her miniscule station inside the FBI van, listening intently to the whispered instructions of the team as they surrounded the suspects' apartment. She tucked her elbows close to make sure she didn't jab the person next to her. Her right leg tingled with pain after putting most of her weight on it. In moments, the almost silent night burst into the sound of frenzied shouting, splintering wood, cries of indignation, and barks of instructions. She heard the doors of adjacent apartments open then slam shut as the residents no doubt saw the swarm of agents wearing jackets emblazoned with FBI.

An eternity elapsed before she heard, "You're up," crackle in her headset. The words she'd been waiting to hear. She knew the FBI had been surveilling these two college students turned cyber terrorists for weeks. The FBI requested her help to take down the computers without allowing the students time to erase anything. Lucinda picked her way over cables and people, her legs protesting after spending so long a time in an awkward position. She grabbed a small satchel and bolted from the van to find an agent inches from the door.

The cool night air slapped her in the face. It felt terrific after being trapped in the stuffy surveillance vehicle.

"Stay to my left and hold on to my vest," the man instructed. In spite of being informed about the escort the combat type gear he wore drove home the potential danger of the operation.

They walked quickly and quietly to the apartment. Her human shield continuously swept the area both visually and with his MK-5 until they reached the apartment door. Once she walked inside, he turned to ensure no one else entered. Having an armed escort even though the suspects had been removed produced an even edgier sensation than when she waited in the van.

"Lucinda, as you insisted the only thing we've done to their computers is dust for prints. Go ahead and do your thing." Shawn, the FBI Agent-in-Charge, motioned her to the dining area. Two computer stations, each with three monitors, stood separated by three servers crammed into the small space.

"Let me know if you need anything from us. We'll be processing the rest of the place." Before she had a chance to respond Shawn turned and gave instructions to the other agents in the room.

Rolling her eyes while his back was turned she knew the comment he'd made had been automatic and meaningless. His attitude came as no surprise since she worked with Shawn on a previous cyber case when she'd been in the army. He'd requested her help to secure the computers during the raid in Columbia, South Carolina. Her current assignment as a civil servant at nearby Ft. Jackson, along with her computer expertise in avoiding logic bombs, made her skills essential in this raid. Lucinda approached the equipment, studying the two setups. They appeared to be identical on the exterior.

She glanced around the adjacent living room of the open plan apartment, noting two brand new gaming chairs facing an equally new seventy-inch television. A makeshift end table consisting of two cardboard boxes sat between the chairs. The table held a dull orange ginger jar lamp that hadn't been in fashion since the 1980s. The once white walls showed a multitude of dings, smudges, and scratches. Posters of scantily clad women of comic book fame graced the walls. Two stacks of unopened boxes stood in a corner which surprised her. One stack held servers while the others contained software cartons. Attached to each item hung a Post-it note with a first name printed on it.

Puzzling over the significance, she sat down at one of the workstations. Lucinda opened her small bag containing several external hard drives. Tuning out all other noise, she set about examining the computers. She didn't want to trip a logic bomb, erasing everything on the hard drive. After spending over two hours to find and eliminate more than twenty traps set by the terrorists on the first computer, she downloaded all the data onto one of the external hard drives. The precaution might not be needed, but these hackers were too savvy not to take the extra step. She stood up to shake out the kinks that had developed during her intense concentration on her task.

The Agent-in-Charge noticed her change in position. "We've finished up our other processing. How are your efforts going?" He handed her a bottle of water.

She felt Shawn's gaze run up and down her body. They'd been on a couple of dates before she'd ended their relationship. At six feet, she towered over a lot of men. Not Shawn. He stood about six foot three inches, making them meet eye-to-eye when she wore her three inch heels. Although he looked great and took interest in her work, something about him told her to be wary. She'd learned the hard way to listen to her inner warning bells.

"Thanks," Lucinda said as she accepted the bottle. "One down, two to go."

Shawn glanced at the equipment. "Two to go? I thought there were only two computers."

"Two desktop computers, but three servers. I started with the system attached to one server. Hard wired. Such a configuration is unusual now days. Next I need to tackle the other computer. What I learned from the first setup should help me with this next one." She squinted at her new target.

"Why the frown?" he asked.

Shaking her head, she responded, "All three servers aren't linked which is odd."

Shawn wrinkled his forehead. "Why should they?"

"More power. All linked together there would be substantially more capacity for whatever they planned to do."

"What is the significance that they aren't linked?"

"At this point, I have no idea. Perhaps after my examination of the other two servers I'll know more." Lucinda waved at the hardware she'd yet to scrutinize.

"Did the first one have the logic bombs you expected?" Shawn asked in a way that indicated his doubt of the concept.

"Yes, it did. Very sophisticated ones. These young men are good at what they do. Very good."

His surprise showed, then he said, "But you're better, right?"

"Exactly. It's why I work for the government." Lucinda wanted the comment to lighten the conversation.

They both knew a lot of the best techs worked for private industry since they paid better. After her four-year stint in the army she decided to apply for a civil service job. She'd been brought on as a co-op where she went to school full-time and worked part-time. Finishing her degree had been her top priority and she had, in a single year. Now she worked full-time for the Department of the Army.

"Is the one computer and server ready for transport?" Shawn queried.

Pausing a moment before answering she finally said, "It should be, but something tells me to leave it until I finish the others."

"Did you copy the content?"

"Of course. Here." Lucinda handed him the external hard drive where she'd stored the code.

"Thanks. I'll give this to our team to dissect." Shawn motioned at one of the techs to take the item and store it with the other evidence.

"Tell them to make another copy before they start," Lucinda suggested.

Making a half turn, Shawn started to give the tech more instructions, but first he said, "Ever the careful one, aren't you?"

"It never hurts to be prepared or suspicious. I think there is more to this than the hacking of the one system we know about." Lucinda decided to give him a heads-up that the culprits might have skimmed money from more than one of the army's weapon systems accounts.

At her pronouncement he turned back, his eyes narrowed and a frown appeared on his forehead. "Did you find something?"

"No, and the absence has me puzzled. I should have found everything."

After her cryptic comment, Lucinda made a trip to the bathroom before settling in behind the other work station. Three more hours passed before Lucinda took another break. That's when she noticed the silence. It spooked her more than the men with assault rifles. The one person remaining in the apartment with her was Shawn. Ignoring the noise earlier, she hadn't noticed when everyone else departed.

"I wondered when you'd come up for air," Shawn said as he put his smart phone away. "You look beat. Do you want to go home and rest awhile before continuing? We'll make sure no one tampers with the equipment until you return."

She stretched and worked out some kinks in her back. "No. I'm getting close and I'd rather finish up now. This is too important."

She clamped down on her nerves. The successful completion of this operation held as much importance to Shawn as it did to her. Perhaps more since he held the position of Agent-in-Charge. He wouldn't make any inappropriate moves. Would he?

Shawn narrowed his eyes at her comment. "You sound worried. What did you find?"

Focusing back on the work, she replied, "A lot of crumbs leading nowhere." Noticing his puzzled look, she explained. "Several sets of code end abruptly for no reason. I think someone deleted a bunch of code to make sure someone like me didn't find the end of the trail."

Shawn huffed out a sigh. "The whole point of setting up this sting the way we did was to make sure no one had time to delete anything."

"Exactly. Whoever did the erasing did so prior to tonight. I'm wondering if these two guys you arrested are patsies."

Shawn's reply came out as a sneer. "So you're saying because there is extra code that stops sharply we didn't catch the real perpetrators?"

Defensive now at his obvious disbelief, Lucinda insisted, "That is one explanation."

"And what would be another?" This time his voice had an edge to it.

"They could have copied code from somewhere else and deleted what they didn't need." Lucinda waved her hands as she became agitated. "Sloppy work."

"Sloppy?" Shawn repeated with eyebrows raised. "So they could be the right guys. Just careless?" Smug confidence indicated his idea was the better explanation.

"They haven't been chaotic with anything else. It seems out of character."

His mistrust of an idea or suggestion not his had been one of the reasons she ended their relationship shortly after the second date.

Again he huffed at her comment. "You know these guys so well you believe some missing code is out of character?"

"I don't know them per se. I understand their code. How they develop each section to perform the way they want. Then how they string everything together."

Lucinda spotted the continuing skepticism in his eyes.

"Their code is different than everyone else's?"

"Each coder is different. Give ten programmers the same task and you'll receive ten different methods of reaching the answer. They'll all work. Some more efficiently than others. A few coders will even add something extra. I've been studying these particular hackers for weeks. I can tell the difference between each of them as well as any other person. It's how I discovered a third programmer."

"You believe there is another programmer involved?" This time Shawn snapped to attention. "Why didn't you say something?"

"I did." Lucinda pointed out the obvious. "That's why I've taken so long and I'm still not done."

"Did you find more logic bombs?"

"Yes, same as the ones on the other setup. I cleared all of them within the first thirty minutes. Since then, I've been trying to figure out how all the extra code worked before portions were deleted."

"Can't you make a copy and take it back to the office?"

"I need to be completely sure there is nothing left to trigger a shut down. If I unplug anything before I'm finished, then the next time the computer boots up a self-destruct process could start." How many times must she explain? She'd repeated the concept every time there'd been a meeting leading up to this raid.

Shawn ran his hand through his hair while grimacing. "I understand. You aren't the only one telling us. We've done things your way so far, so go ahead and finish."

Irritated at his continued nonacceptance of reality, she spat out, "You don't need to wait on me. The guards are still outside, aren't they?" At his nod, she continued. "Then I'll be fine. If you want, I'll call when I'm done."

"No, I'll stick with you."

Knowing two armed men stood outside helped convince her Shawn wouldn't try anything sexual. She composed herself. Once again Lucinda had something to drink and made a trip to the bathroom before she continued. After another two hours, she finally said, "Done. I'm as confident as I can be the systems are all clear."

"Good. I'm exhausted and all I've done is watch you work. You must be dead on your feet." His voice sounded more conciliatory than their earlier conversation.

She pulled out another external hard drive and started the copy process. She used a total of three hard drives to store all the data. "While I work I don't notice how tired I am, but once I stop, look out. I might do a face plant walking to the parking lot." When the copy process completed, Lucinda proceeded to shut down the systems.

"I'll take the backups directly to the office and let the other techs see what they can find. I can drop you at your place."

Noticing his eyes remained on her face and didn't venture lower, she understood the information interested him more than she did at the moment. Lucinda didn't hear any warning bells, so agreed. "Thanks. I'll take you up on the offer. Make sure the original machines are kept intact. Someone needs to see if they can recover the deleted code. I can do the work if your team doesn't have the expertise or time."

"You've completed your assigned task. Anything else will be done by FBI technicians."

Lucinda ached to continue the project, but knew FBI procedures. Requesting Shawn to assign the task to her was futile. Besides, asking a favor might give him the idea she wanted to work with him. Not the message she intended to send.

As promised, Shawn dropped her at her apartment and sped away to FBI headquarters. Good. She'd started to second-guess her decision so, she felt relief when he didn't offer to walk her to the door.

The one-story climb to her apartment almost did her in. She couldn't remember the last time she'd been so exhausted. Once inside her apartment, she slid the three dead bolts into place and checked the windows to make sure they were still secure. Even when sleep-deprived, she didn't let her guard down until she completed her security check. Knowing the neighborhood was safe didn't lessen her need for extra measures. There had been a time when she hadn't been safe even behind locked doors. Never again.

With her routine accomplished, she stripped off her clothes, letting them fall to the floor as she walked to the shower. The hot water felt so good she almost dropped off. "Wash your hair then you can sleep for the rest of the day," she commanded. Talking out loud kept her awake so she continued. "Almost done. Dry off. Blow dry your hair enough to stop the dripping. Good. Put on your sleep T-shirt. Done." She walked the few steps to her bed and collapsed on top, not bothering to pull back the covers.

Four hours later, she jerked awake and bolted upright at the pounding on her door. "Why the hell is someone banging on my door?" Glancing at her clock, she noticed twelve o'clock glared back. Noon or midnight? She had no idea since blackout linings on her curtains kept the room dark.

Having the presence of mind to grab a pair of yoga pants before making her way to the door, she yelled, "Okay, okay, I'm coming. Hold on." She stuffed her legs into the pants as she half hopped and jerked her way to the entrance.

"Who the hell is knocking on my door?" She mumbled to herself. Looking through the peep hole she gasped at the sight of the man standing there.

The decadent but definitely unwanted Jason Meyers stood on the other side of the door. He'd been the one who alerted the FBI about the penetration into the army's accounting programs for various weapon systems. They worked in the same government building although in different departments.

"It's me. Jason. Jason Meyers." He glanced over his shoulder as if expecting someone to sneak up behind him. "Let me in. I found something important."

CHAPTER TWO

After several minutes the door cracked open with the safety chain attached. "What do you want, Jason?"

Her intense glare would normally have stopped him from further speech. "To talk about the raid. The FBI missed something."

She closed the door long enough to begrudgingly remove the safety chain and opened it a few inches.

"Thanks." Jason slipped into Lucinda's apartment through the small opening. Once shut she put the deadbolts back in place as he peered out the window adjacent to the entrance. After looking through all the windows in the room he turned to face her, trying to hide his grin. "Oh, sorry, I guess I woke you."

He hadn't considered the fact she'd be in bed at noon. The normally perfect Lucinda looked almost scary. Scary as a puppy recently pulled out of the river. Her hair had spikes going in all directions. No makeup, not that she needed it. Then the stare. The one that made most men stop in their tracks. The look made you assume she knew what you were thinking. Didn't like the thoughts. Planned to kill you for thinking it.

"What gave you the first clue?" Lucinda's snarky response came out in a snap. She turned and clomped to the kitchen. "Sit down. I'm making coffee. Don't speak until I drink at least one cup."

"Sorry, I ..." Jason wanted to explain the reason he'd arrived without prior warning.

She held up her hand and gave him the stare again. "I said wait. I mean it. No talking."

Not having another choice, he sat on her couch and waited. He looked around her living room. Having worked in the same building with her for more than a year, he noticed she wore conservative, tailored clothing which made him think her house would reflect the same image. On the other hand, when a group of people from their offices had gone out together to a few clubs she'd worn some sexy, flirty clothes in wild colors.

Her furnishings represented the combination of those two styles. Pale grey walls, a couch of darker grey, several red and yellow pillows with ruffles and sparkly stuff thrown around kept the room from being dreary. He appreciated the mega size of the couch. With his six-foot-five-inch frame he seldom sat on a couch where his knees didn't stick up and almost hit his chin. Several oil paintings hung on the wall. He'd seen similar ones at the starving artist sales so he knew the sunflower painting wasn't a real Van Gogh. The one thing separating the living room from the kitchen was a breakfast bar with red placemats, coffee maker, and toaster. Yellow curtains graced the window.

Apparently she had a Keurig since she returned to the living room moments later, taking a deep swallow of coffee. She gave him an evil look and held up her hand to make sure he wouldn't start talking.

"Do you want a cup of coffee or tea?" she finally asked.

"No, thanks. Not right now." He waited for her to join him. With a great deal of effort he tried not to look at her breasts. She'd probably slept in the T-shirt so there was nothing underneath. The fact he could see the color of her nipples through the shirt caused a reaction making him uncomfortable, literally. The thought made him realize she'd also be minus any underwear beneath her yoga pants. Clearing his throat, he looked at the Van Gogh-like painting over her head until she sat down in the chair opposite.

"Explain why you woke me out of a sound sleep." Lucinda's voice came out in a husky growl.

"I found something. Something that couldn't wait." His voice sounded like gravel even to himself. He cleared his throat and paused a moment. "What time did you finish last night?"

At that moment he realized she might not have had much sleep. His boss told him about the successful raid. However, he had no idea how long the event had taken.

"I returned to my apartment about eight o'clock this morning. What is this something?"

He noticed her eyes had gone from glaring at him to interest. "Oh, double sorry then. But I thought my information too important to wait." He hadn't apologized to anyone this much in a long time. Well, not ever, really.

"What? Tell me already."

"I found a money trail." He'd been so proud of his discovery until he'd realized the people responsible would kill him and Lucinda if they thought they'd been outed by one or both of them. Thinking about the possibility kept nagging at him. Only forced concentration on his part kept the idea from overwhelming him. He figured he could take care of himself, but the thought of anyone else in danger didn't sit well with him. Especially a woman.

Lucinda's brow knitted in annoyance as she stood and returned to the kitchen. He assumed she needed another cup of coffee.

She spoke from the kitchen. "Money. We know. They did this whole thing for the money. To finance their terror plot. Whatever the plan is." Lucinda sounded aggravated.

"No, no. Not *that* money," Jason insisted.

Moments later she sat back down with her fresh cup of coffee. "Explain."

"We already knew about the money discovered a few weeks ago. I even tracked how they spent it." As a budget analyst for the army at Ft. Jackson, Jason had access to most of the financial systems where resources were tracked for the multi-million dollar weapons used by the military. "I didn't see any evidence of terrorist-type items like guns, explosives, those sorts of things. So I started digging deeper."

"Did they buy a bunch of servers and software with the first batch of money?" Lucinda's eyes remained intent on his as she sipped from her mug and leaned forward.

Her question startled him. "Yes. How did you know?"

With a shrug she explained, "I saw them in the apartment."

So there were extra servers in the apartment. How were they being used? "When I told the FBI they figured the computers would all be hooked up together. Were they?"

"No, that's the odd part." Lucinda pursed her lips as she sat back. "Still in boxes with Post-it notes on each one, containing a single name."

He sat up straight. "What? Unopened boxes of computer stuff doesn't make sense. What kind of names? Company names?" What could these people be doing with them? Maybe they infected the equipment with some kind of virus? Give them the ability to sneak in undetected?

"It is strange. First names like Matt, John, Bubba, whatever." She shrugged in an exaggerated manor. "We'll talk about them in a minute. What money, if not the funds purchasing this stuff?"

"They've siphoned funds from several of the weapon systems we monitor."

"What?" Lucinda shot up from her chair. "That's what I was afraid might happen. I didn't realize it already had."

"Now you understand why I'm here." He folded his arms across his chest. Keeping his mind on their conversation became more difficult. Her reaction caused her unfettered breasts to bounce and draw his attention. This was not the time or place he told himself. Part of his anatomy didn't agree.

"Did you report your findings to your boss?" She settled back into her chair, but looked a lot more interested in what he had to say. She tucked one leg under her with the other one on the floor in front of her, tapping at a rapid beat.

Jason struggled to keep looking at her face. "I placed a call to my boss, Mr. Anderson, but he'd left early for lunch. Then I started thinking about the repercussions. So I decided to leave and come here."

She frowned at him. "Repercussions? What do you mean?"

"They've gone further into our systems than we previously understood."

"True. And?"

He needed to make sure she understood the danger. "How did they manage to penetrate to that level without us knowing? What else have they done? Are they tapping our office phones, our workstations? How did they acquire the passwords? I wanted to talk to you before telling Mr. Anderson. After he's advised, he'll begin an investigation with tons of people knowing about it. I figured if we control who has knowledge about this...this—" He threw up his hands not knowing what to call the intrusion. "Whatever they've accessed then we might be able to shut down the siphoning of funds before they take more. If these bad guys think they've been discovered, what will keep them from taking all the rest of the money before we can figure out how to stop them? I needed someone to talk to about the options. Someone who knows more about the technology. I know about the systems, where the money is kept from a user perspective and can follow it, but I don't know how to trace the computer code like you do."

Lucinda stood up and paced the floor. "So you think they took more money? Enough money to maybe fund a big terrorist attack? Not buy some extra hardware and software." He nodded when she glanced at him. "I agree with your logic. And the danger. We could be in real trouble." She continued her walk around the living room.

He felt relieved she understood his concerns. "So how do we go about learning more? Can the code you looked at today provide us more information?"

Lucinda stopped her wandering and slapped her hand on her forehead. "That's it! That's what I couldn't decipher last night."

Jason frowned, not understanding. "You already found something?"

"Extra code. I found some extra code that ended abruptly as if someone didn't want us to track it to the final phase. They should have deleted everything. Guess they ran out of time."

His frown deepened. "I thought you designed the takedown to make sure they couldn't delete anything."

"We did, we did. Someone performed the partial deletions before last night. I also found evidence of at least one other coder." Her excitement showed in her face along with the concern.

"What? You mean there could be more than the two guys they arrested last night?"

"Exactly. I told Shawn Murphy, he's the FBI Agent-in-Charge."

"I know who he is. Mr. Anderson and I spoke with him about the initial problem after I reported it. The one that spawned last night's raid." Shawn had become a fixture at his office. Some of the other men in his branch had worked with him on some hot project a few years before Jason arrived. Now they hung out together.

"I didn't know what the missing subroutines meant, but you may have discovered the reason. The code going nowhere is important. You've provided a possible explanation."

He blew out a deep breath and slumped back on the couch in defeat. "If the program segments were deleted, then how can you figure out what happens next?"

"It's tricky, but not impossible." Her expression turned pensive. "I've turned everything over to the FBI and their analysts. They tasked me to eliminate any logic bombs the guys set. That's what I did last night."

"Logic bombs?" The only kind of bombs Jason knew about blew up stuff like buildings and people. Lucinda couldn't mean that kind.

"It's something hackers create to delete everything if someone they don't want to access their code finds a way in," Lucinda explained. "These guys took caution to a new level. They set up four different types of traps."

Jason couldn't help but be impressed. "You figured out how to keep the code intact?"

"Yes. It's my expertise." She gave him a saucy grin. "A trick I learned in my misspent youth."

He couldn't help grinning back at her. She might be blonde, but she certainly wasn't the stereotypical dumb blonde. "So the FBI won't allow you additional access?" If she wasn't allowed to continue her search, how would they unearth the truth?

"Not the original plan. I did mention to Shawn I found some code abruptly stopping in the middle of nowhere."

"Do you think he'll tell the FBI techs to look into it?" Jason wanted to be in on the find. His initial investigation had uncovered the problem; it was his right to be part of the solution.

Shrugging her shoulders, she frowned. "He didn't seem to think my observations important so he may not."

Jason urged her to continue with a roll of his hand. "Then he might let you work with them on a specific piece? Like the one you told him about?"

"Maybe." She gave him a look that didn't inspire confidence.

"You could use your womanly wiles to make him do what you want," Jason joked. "I've seen the way he looks at you."

Now she glared at him. "Not funny, Meyers. Not my style." She stomped off to the kitchen.

He realized how much he sounded like a jerk as soon as the words had come out of his mouth. "Hey, I wouldn't ask if this wasn't important." The last thing he wanted to do was alienate her. He followed her into the kitchen. "If you think of a better plan, I'm all for it."

She jerked her thumb toward the coffee options as she set about making another cup of coffee for herself. "Go ahead, pick out what you want. There are all kinds of tea, hot chocolate, and coffee."

"What the heck? I might as well have the jitters for a week." After all the coffee he'd already consumed today the extra caffeine would keep him wired for a long time. She seemed to have forgiven him for his stupid comment. Jason selected a dark roast. For some reason he thought about the number of times he and his mother enjoyed a hot drink while discussing serious topics. He'd started out with hot chocolate and graduated to coffee. Shaking his head at the random thought of his mother, he focused on Lucinda.

She glanced at him as she pushed the brew button. "Exactly."

He picked out a mug from the selection on the counter. "So how do you think we can find out more about the code you found? Is there anything I can do? Like tell Shawn I need more information or something?"

She perked up at his comment. "Could you ask Shawn without your boss knowing?"

"Probably. He's given me full rein on this project. There are a lot of other assignments he's working on to keep him occupied."

"What about the fact you wanted to speak to him today? Isn't he going to call you back or stop by your desk?" She led the way as they returned to the living room.

"Yes, he will." He sat down on the couch. "I'll come up with something. Don't worry about him. Will my request to Shawn be of any help?" He didn't see how his asking would make a difference. "You'll need to tell me exactly what to ask to make sure you obtain the information we need."

Sitting back down on the chair, she curled both her feet under her. "Contact Shawn. I'll give you his number. Tell him you spoke to me and I told you about the code leading to nowhere. Explain you want to see if anything matches up in some of the other computer systems you handle. Also, clarify that I need the original computer to find out if the code that's been deleted can be restored. You're trying to be proactive to make sure nothing else has been corrupted."

Puzzled, he asked, "Didn't you basically spell out the same thing to him?"

"Yes, but if the plea comes from you he'll be more likely to give credence to the request."

He set his mug on the coffee table. "No problem. I'll call when I return to the office."

"Probably need to wait until tomorrow. Otherwise he'll wonder why we talked since I'm not in the office today."

"Right. Good idea."

She tilted her head. "So why all the cloak-and-dagger stuff when you showed up a little while ago?"

"Oh, that." He felt his face turning red. "Well, maybe I'm a little paranoid, but I thought if someone figured out a way to siphon off so much money, then they'd be watching to see if we caught on."

"You mean if you found the information by looking at specific areas of the financial system your access would somehow notify the terrorists?" Her feet hit the floor as she asked the question.

"Exactly."

"That would be another form of a logic bomb. One you wouldn't know you'd tripped." Lucinda started pacing the floor again.

He shrugged, unsure how to avoid something he didn't know existed. "So what should I do?"

"The question is, what should *we* do?" She placed her coffee adjacent to Jason's.

He rolled his eyes. "If you want to split hairs, okay, what do we do?"

She grinned at him. "As a budget analyst, they might figure you're harmless unless you find something else."

"True. That's why I came to see you." He tried not to be insulted with her calling him harmless. He felt his manhood had been attacked. So what was her point? He tried to concentrate on the computer issues.

"Yes, well, I've already been exploring things."

"And they know it." Worried all over again for her safety, he wondered if he should have involved her. At that moment he swore to himself he'd keep her safe. Whatever it took.

"Yes, I'm sure they do if what you suspect is true. There are more hackers than the two college kids arrested last night."

He noticed her frown. He reached over and touched her hand to reassure her. "I made sure no one followed me from work."

Pulling her hand away, she asked, "When did you make your discovery?"

"Earlier today." He sat back on the couch, wondering why she'd become so remote.

"I'm sure they are doing everything electronically. So they probably didn't have time to set up cameras or vehicles to follow you. They won't connect the two of us unless we are seen together at the office or work on the same set of code at the same time. We'll need to be careful from now on."

"Understood. Should we talk on the phone?" He didn't want her in danger, but he didn't trust anyone else to help him discover if more illegal penetrations into the systems had occurred. Not to mention tracking any money siphoned out.

Tilting her head, she seemed to consider the question before answering. "Maybe, but let's not call from our work phones. Since they're government property they can be monitored. We have no idea who has access to the recordings. We might be wise to buy some throw-away phones and use those to talk to each other."

He picked up his now cold coffee and took a sip. "I'll buy two on my way back to the office. If you're not planning to go to work today, I can drop one off at your cubicle. Do you have a desk drawer you keep unlocked?"

"Yes. Put the phone in the center drawer. I keep office supplies there. Shove the phone to the back and I'll pick it up tomorrow. Plug in the phone number of yours under the listing of, well, not your real name." She paused a moment to consider. "We should use some kind of code names. What do you want to use?"

"If we use someone's real name they could end up in trouble." After a moment of thought he grinned mischievously. Maybe a little teasing would help ease the tension they both felt at their overwhelming task. "How about cuddle-bear and sweet-baby?"

Her famous stare reappeared. "Really? You want me to call you cuddle-bear?" Lucinda's scorn was evident in her tone.

He chuckled. "Okay, I know it sounds stupid. However, if we need to phone when someone else is around and don't want them to know who is calling then using those names will make them think we're talking to a girlfriend or boyfriend. Not some co-conspirator." Although he tried to lighten their discussion, he didn't want either of them to lose sight of the seriousness of their situation.

Lucinda rolled her eyes. "Fine. The best I can do is call you Bear and I'll be Baby." Shaking her head, she took another sip of coffee. "If any of my friends hear me, they'll think I need to be committed."

"Same here." He shrugged. "If you can think of something better, I'm all for it."

"No, you're right. We don't want to use anyone's real name in case we're being observed or recorded. So we also need to be careful how we phrase things."

"You're right. Maybe we can work on some code words." He liked the idea of being a master spy. His chest puffed up with the mere thought.

She pursed her lips and gave him a stern look. "Let's not get too carried away. We'll stick with the names for now. No frequent contact even with the phones. If you need to tell me something, then write a note and put it in the drawer I mentioned. I'll put a birthday card inside an envelope. Slip the paper inside. Most people will ignore a card during a search." She'd used the ploy in her high school days when trying to keep nosey people out of her business.

"Great idea. I'll do the same. I'll use the top drawer of the filing cabinet which doesn't lock like the others. I keep the office party supplies in there."

"Party supplies?" Her eyebrows rose.

"Yeah, like paper plates and napkins and the Happy Birthday sign we hang up across a cubicle of the lucky person."

"How did you end up with those?"

Jason replied with a shrug. "Inherited the filing cabinet with all the contents. I tried giving the stuff away, but no takers. Now I'm stuck."

She made an unladylike snort. "Lucky you. Fair enough. Go ahead and return to the office. Maybe you better write down your address in case I need to find you."

"Right." He scribbled his address and apartment number on a notepad she provided along with a pen.

"Call me later tonight," she instructed, then gave him the stare again. "Not before eight o'clock. I want to catch a little more sleep. I'll reach out to some people who might know if anyone has been recruiting hackers."

"You know people like that?" He'd been right to contact her. Not only did she understand computers she knew hackers. They might be needed to solve this mystery. But how exactly did she know these people?

CHAPTER THREE

If she crawled back in bed now she'd never manage to sleep tonight. Deciding to take another shower to help wake up, she stepped into the bathroom. Seeing herself in the mirror, she blurted, "Oh, my God! You've been sitting in the living room talking to a man when you look like that?"

Her hair stood up like a porcupine with a few quills missing. She remembered too late she'd washed her hair, and then crashed before it had time to dry completely. No makeup and she wore a T-shirt so old she could see through the material. Lord. She appreciated the fact Jason had been a gentleman and not commented or looked overlong at her breasts. At least not that she'd noticed.

She'd revealed more than intended. She didn't hate the idea of him seeing her nearly naked. When she'd observed him working out in the gym next to their office building she'd fantasized what he looked like without a shirt. Or anything at all.

Forget the notion, she scolded. Wipe the idea out of your head. She didn't need to continue daydreaming. Once finished with her shower and dressing routine, she recognized the need for food. Rummaging through her refrigerator and tiny pantry, she found the makings for an omelet and toast. This time she chose to drink milk instead of coffee. She'd had way too much caffeine during the last twenty-four hours.

Feeling human again, she decided to reach out to some people she'd not contacted in a long time. Logging on to her laptop in her guest room/office, she lost herself in the world of hackers. Having been one in her teens, she periodically reconnected since they could provide information no government source ever would. None of them knew about her new life, only her reformation. She'd never ratted any of them out so her welcome stayed intact. After two hours of online chatting and sending a few emails, she felt satisfied at least one or two of her queries would be answered.

With the serious task accomplished, she gave her friend, Marcella, a ring to see if she had plans for dinner. The two of them worked together until Marcella accepted a promotion in another organization at Ft. Jackson. They hadn't seen each other in a while and Lucinda missed their chats.

Marcella, always the jokester, answered the phone. "Hey girl, I heard you singlehandedly brought down a terrorist cell."

Lucinda couldn't help but grin at the outrageous comment. "You know it, girlfriend." They both laughed. "Seriously, things went exactly as the FBI planned. I did a small part, but what a rush."

"Small part? You unmasked those guys."

"How did you hear about it?"

"Something like that makes the rounds in a flash when one of our own is a significant player. Were the terrorists hot?" Marcella always had sex on her mind.

Lucinda let out a very unladylike snort. "Hardly, they were a couple of skinny, nerdy college kids."

She heard Marcella sigh heavily. "Well, how disappointing."

"We can talk all about this over dinner. That's why I called. I thought you might want to meet for dinner tonight."

"Any excuse not to cook is my idea of a great plan. How about six o'clock at the new German restaurant?"

"You bet. I hope they make a good jaeger schnitzel." The thought of mushrooms and brown gravy over a crispy schnitzel made Lucinda's mouth water.

"I can taste the pan fried potatoes now. Hey, I need to finish up this report, so we'll talk later." She disconnected before Lucinda could say goodbye.

Lucinda chuckled at the typical Marcella response. She loved to gossip, but business came first during working hours.

After the last twenty-four hours Lucinda looked forward to some girl talk. The constant need to prove her abilities within her chosen field took a toll. To relax and discuss nothing more important than the latest fashion felt like a luxury right now. It would help clear her head so she would be able to focus better after the break. Besides, the two of them enjoyed each other's company.

With more than an hour to spare Lucinda decided to do some additional work. *I'll check to see if anyone responded to my emails. Some of those people do nothing but surf the net and chat online.*

One response sat in her inbox.

CHAPTER FOUR

Jason checked repeatedly to see if someone followed him. He didn't have any experience spotting a tail, but he'd seen enough cop shows to have a general idea of how to lose one. Before stopping to buy the throw-away phones, he used what knowledge he had. He also made sure to buy the phones from different stores using cash. Not sure if the extra step was necessary, but hoped the effort would at least slow down anyone who might be looking.

Arriving back at the office, he did his best to return to his routine. He'd made up a question for Mr. Anderson to explain his earlier request for a meeting. Although Mr. Anderson gave him a perplexed look at his feeble attempt, there didn't seem to be any red flags. Once most of the other personnel left for the day he slipped Lucinda's throw-away phone where they'd agreed.

Feeling pleased with his accomplishments, he stopped at a local civil servant hangout for a beer before heading home.

"Jason, my man, you don't come here often. Celebrating something?" Bob, one of his coworkers, slapped him on the back.

"End of a work day. What else would I be celebrating? You? I'm guessing you've been here a while," Jason commented.

"Yes, I have. Something big to celebrate. And, yes, I've been here a while." The man made exaggerated nods of agreement.

He couldn't help but grin at Bob's unusual state. "What's the good news?"

"I'm going to be a daddy." He puffed out his chest and gave a silly smile.

"Congratulations, Bob. Let me buy you another beer." Jason raised a hand to the bartender indicating another drink for the man.

"See, that's what happens every time I tell someone." He swayed toward the bar. "Glad I didn't tell everyone while still at work. I'd have missed out on all the free beer."

Jason moved toward the end of the bar where several seats stood vacant. Most people huddled around Bob, giving him advice on raising a child. Jason knew he had nothing to offer so he sat alone, thinking. Bob seemed proud and pleased about the upcoming birth of his progeny. Jason hadn't given much thought to being a parent until now. The idea of having a child with Lucinda sprang to mind. Hold on a minute. They weren't even dating. Don't get carried away. Stop thinking like that. For now.

Nursing his beer, he watched as people entered and left the bar trying to decide if anybody had followed him. He focused on a man of slight build, about five feet eight inches, Asian. About the time he decided the man was indeed watching him, an Asian woman entered the bar and headed directly for the man. He stood and embraced her before they sat and plunged into a deep conversation. Shaking his head, Jason decided he was being paranoid. Paying his bill, he left and headed home.

He didn't notice the man and woman he'd spotted in the bar follow him in a van.

His apartment seemed empty and devoid of comfort. This wasn't the first time he'd felt that way when arriving home. Although the trailer where he'd spent his adolescence hadn't been grandiose, it had been warm and welcoming. Probably due to his mother's presence. Why had memories of his mother been plaguing him today? Maybe she wanted him to know she kept watch over him while he performed the dangerous job. The moment the notion occurred to him, he felt wrapped in a warm embrace. He smiled at the idea then shook off the fanciful thoughts. Taking a deep breath he resolved to be the tough guy his fraternity brothers thought he was.

He wandered into the kitchen and opened the refrigerator. He stared at the contents, hoping for inspiration on what to make for dinner. Not sure if thoughts of his mother or the desire for comfort food made him decide on homemade mac-n-cheese. One of the first things she'd taught him how to fix.

Midway through its preparation, his phone rang.

"Hey, Bud, you have plans for the weekend?" his friend asked.

"Yep. Football. I'm tailgating with some Frat brothers. What've you got goin' on?" Jason continued to work on his dinner while he carried on the conversation.

"I have a date with a new chick and she has an outstanding roommate. I wanted to give you an opportunity to join us for a good time."

He grinned. "Thanks for the offer, but no." He knew his friend too well to fall for his line. "I remember the last time you suckered me into a double date. You called her hot. Not sure how you define hot and outstanding, but it's not the same as me."

Jason placed the bowl of pasta and cheese in the oven. While the mac-n-cheese cooked, he decided to put together a salad and reached in the refrigerator for lettuce, tomatoes, and cucumber.

His friend's voice changed to a plea. "Oh, man. Come on. This chick won't go out alone with me. She insists on a double date since it's our first."

"So you haven't even seen her roommate, right?"

Following a silent pause his friend finally replied. "Busted. No. I haven't. I'd owe you big time. Do it for me?"

More pleading made Jason feel uncomfortable. "If I didn't already have plans with my brothers, I'd go," Jason said although he knew he lied. About the plans for tailgating and the fact he'd go on the date in other circumstances.

"Next time?" His friend seemed resigned.

"Sure." Jason agreed, but he'd make certain he had other plans then as well.

While he finished chopping stuff for the salad, he decided to put the ingredients of his mother's lasagna on his shopping list. Maybe he'd ask Lucinda over for dinner. No, they didn't need to be seen together. Scratch the idea. After several minutes, he couldn't shake the notion. If she was careful not to be followed, she could park on the other side of the complex. A few women from their office lived over there if she needed an excuse. Then she could come here and they could talk more about what she found on the computers. Of course, everything depended on whether Shawn gave her permission. From memory, he made the grocery list and set it aside – just in case.

CHAPTER FIVE

Marcella and Lucinda tucked into their schnitzels with enthusiasm.

"I'll need to spend another five hours at the gym for eating this," Marcella said then groaned.

"But it's worth it, right?" Lucinda grinned.

Giving a shrug, she said, "I'll let you know once I've finished my penance. You know the worst part?"

"There's a worst part?" Lucinda put another forkful in her mouth.

Sticking her tongue out first, Marcella then replied, "Yeah, there is. I know you won't need to."

Pretending offense, Lucinda raised her eyebrows and gave her a hard look. "I think I spend enough time at the gym."

"Exactly. You work out almost every day then eat like a pig."

"Hey, I don't eat like this every day."

Marcella pouted. "I know, I know. Neither do I, but somehow the results aren't the same for me."

"What can I say?" Lucinda shrugged. "High metabolism."

"That's why I hate you." Marcella grinned to show she didn't really mean the statement.

"Keep up the snarky talk and I won't share my big adventure with you."

Obviously contrite, Marcella continued. "You know I'm kidding, right?"

"Of course I do. Now, let me fill you in on the exciting life of an Information Assurance Manager." Lucinda related the tale of the raid. She tried to make the mundane work sound somewhat interesting.

Marcella threw up her hands at the end. "That's all? You sat there for hours working on those computers?"

Lucinda grinned at her friend's reaction. "What can I say? It's what I do."

"I expected something interesting. Not…not…well, not that," she said with a huff. "At least the FBI agents could have smacked the terrorists around or something."

"I believe that would be considered police brutality," Lucinda pointed out.

"At least the action would sound more exciting. And you said the terrorists were simply college nerds." Marcella gave a loud sigh, put both elbows on the table and rested her chin on her upturned palms.

"Yep. That about sums it up."

"Then I suppose I'm not jealous anymore." Taking another sip of wine, she must have thought of another angle. "Wait a minute. What did the FBI agent look like?"

Not looking at her, Lucinda downplayed his importance. "You know him. Shawn. I introduced you to him."

Marcella sat up straight and put her hands in her lap. "Ohhh, yes, I remember Shawn. He's a hunk." She leaned forward expecting to hear something more interesting.

"I admit he is good-looking. We went out twice. Not my type." Lucinda made chopping motions with her hand.

Letting out a moan, Marcella replied, "What is your type, Lucinda? You don't go out much and when you do, you call a halt after two dates. What's wrong with Shawn?"

Still not looking at her friend, Lucinda said, "I'm not sure. There is a bad vibe when I'm around him."

At the same time her mind wandered to thoughts of Jason. Would she call a halt after two dates with him? She didn't immediately say yes. That came as a surprise.

"Bad vibe? Are you kidding me? You are impossible." Marcella set her wine glass down hard enough to make the remaining liquid slosh in the glass.

Lucinda didn't want to discuss Shawn anymore, or think about Jason. "Enough about me. How is your new job?"

"I'm really liking it. I have my own team and my new boss is fantastic. He listens to my suggestions and we've developed a plan together for our department. Of course, he doesn't agree with everything I say." Marcella gave her a smug look before saying, "Not yet at least."

Lucinda chuckled at her comment. "That is fantastic. I couldn't be happier for you. Your talents were not used to their full capacity in our shop." She meant every word. Marcella deserved the promotion and recognition.

"So you told me. I'm glad you pushed me to apply for the new position. I'd become so frustrated I didn't enjoy going to work."

"At our age something like that can make you quit or do something that will harm your future with civil service. Neither is a good option."

"Again, thanks for suggesting the change."

"You'd do the same for me."

"Your right, I would."

They smiled at each other in recognition of their personal and professional closeness.

After catching up with each other they left the restaurant together, each climbing into their own vehicles. As they drove off, neither noticed the white sedan following Lucinda.

CHAPTER SIX

Jason sat in front of the television to eat his solitary dinner. He'd recorded a re-run of *CSI Cyber* the night before to watch while he ate. Engrossed in the possibilities of what hackers could do, he jumped at the sound of the throw-away phone ringing. He'd set the alarm to make sure he called Lucinda. After eight o'clock.

He paused the program on television and placed the call to her regular cell phone since she didn't have the throw away yet. He'd have to remember to not give away anything important in case someone listened. When she picked up he said, "Hey, Baby, it's me. Did you miss me?" Irritating her made him chuckle.

He heard her growl before saying, "I've been too busy, Bear," in a sickeningly sweet voice he'd never heard her use.

Her tone changed to professional. "I've been chatting with old musician friends all afternoon to see if they received invitations to play at the special concert." Her voice sounded serious.

It didn't take Jason more than a moment to understand that musician meant hackers so concert must be her word for the computer code. She knew some hackers who could have been approached to do the job. That must be what she meant.

"Did anybody you know play at the concert?"

"A mutual friend suggested the name of someone who bragged about an invitation."

"It would be great to know if he participated." Jason became excited at the possibility of a lead on the hacker. He managed to keep his reply calm. "Then we could invite him to our party."

"I decided the same thing," Lucinda agreed. "I'll let you know if he's interested after I speak to him."

Remembering the promise he'd made to himself he asked, "I can make the call if you'd rather." He didn't want her to be in danger.

"That's okay, I'll ask. If we decide to proceed with the party, then I think the two of us should go hear some of his music to make sure we want him to play for us."

Good. She wouldn't attempt a face-to-face without him. At least he thought that's what she told him. The more he considered her coming to his apartment to discuss all the options, the better he liked the idea. He didn't want a misunderstanding to mess up this investigation.

"Great idea. I'll wait for your call." He disconnected.

He decided to write a note to put in Lucinda's desk drawer. The letter took a minute to compose. Being careful not to mention anything incriminating, he changed the wording twice. Reread the message several more times to make sure the phrasing made sense. Once satisfied he printed the missive on a fresh sheet of paper. No sense taking chances someone would recognize his handwriting.

> *Baby,*
>
> *When you have something to tell me, give me a call and we'll schedule a dinner date. At my place. My mother's lasagna.*
>
> *Love Ya*
> *Bear*

The salutation would irritate her. He grinned.

CHAPTER SEVEN

Lucinda opened her desk drawer the next day to look around for the phone. Jason had placed it exactly where she suggested. She also noticed a folded piece of paper under it. She'd brought a card to add to the drawer for future use. Once she finished reading the directive, a grin stole onto her lips without her consent. A small sigh escaped at the idea of homemade lasagna. So tempting. They needed to talk about her call to make sure he understood the meaning. He'd been right, although the notion galled her to admit it. They needed to come up with a simple code. Like calling the hackers musicians.

She'd work on the code before calling him. And she wanted to wait until she heard from Shawn. Assuming he'd contact her. If he didn't, Lucinda had no idea what to do next. She put the phone into her purse and the note into the shredder. No sense taking chances.

One of Lucinda's coworkers popped into her cubicle and startled her. "Hey, girl, welcome back to the mundane world. How was the special assignment?"

"Not as special as you would think. The work is similar to what we do every day."

"Really? I thought working with the FBI would be fascinating."

She shrugged her shoulders. "Just another government job."

"Well, burst my bubble." A pout appeared on her coworker's pretty face.

"Sorry. How'd things go here yesterday?"

"Same old, same old. Guess I better head back to work."

Lucinda wanted to keep anyone else from finding out the details. The fewer who knew, the fewer in danger. Plus, those who didn't know could be eliminated from involvement. She couldn't shake the idea someone among her fellow coworkers might be spying on them. And helping terrorists crack their systems.

Wait, was it possible that woman was one of them? Someone involved in hacking their systems? Had she been trying to find out how much Lucinda knew and how much she guessed?

Determined to be more aware of people as they approached, she rearranged her cubicle to allow visibility of anyone before they stepped into the space.

Lucinda concentrated on the routine work in an effort to not fret about whether Shawn would contact her or not.

Shortly before lunch the phone rang for the millionth time. "Information Security, Lucinda speaking."

"Hey, gorgeous. How about meeting me for lunch?"

Lucinda recognized Shawn's voice. *Was he flirting or did he plan to tell her she could work on the project?* "Hello, Shawn. Thanks for the invitation, but I'll be working through lunch to catch up after being gone yesterday."

"Ouch. Does that mean I can't ask for any favors?"

Lucinda frowned, still unsure as to his intent. "Depends on the favor."

"I received a call from Jason Meyers. You know him?"

"I know who he is. He works in Budget." She didn't want to give any indication of the importance of the call.

"He said you two talked."

"We did. I mentioned the subroutine that stopped abruptly. Since the code was imbedded in a system that controls his project, I thought he might have some insight."

"Apparently your comment piqued his interest. He'd like you to follow up and see what else you can find. I spoke to your boss. She gave the go-ahead. You can spend half your time working on it."

Lucinda tried to downplay her enthusiasm. "Fine. I'll check with my boss to see how long she wants me to work on this." Inside she did a fist pump and a celebratory dance.

"Unless you find something within the week, I doubt we'll go further. I'll have one of our techs bring you the computers. They're finished with what they need."

"I'll see what I can do. Thanks for calling." Lucinda hung up before he could try anymore flirting. Now the inside of her stomach felt like a hamster was running full out on its wheel.

One week. That wasn't much time. I'll make copies to an external hard drive. Perhaps I can obtain permission to work from home on it if time runs out. The actual computer will tell me more, but I'll make the copies in case I have to turn the original back to the FBI before I finish. With her plan made, she went back to her regular work to complete her tasks as quickly as possible to be ready when the computers arrived.

With about an hour's worth of routine work left to do her boss, Marge, arrived at Lucinda's desk along with a technician carrying one of the confiscated computers. "Your buddy at the FBI said he planned to call you to tell you about this new request."

Motioning the tech to put the computer on the desk where she'd cleared a space she addressed Marge. "Well, I wouldn't call him my buddy, but yes, Shawn did give me a heads-up."

Marge gave her a knowing look. "It doesn't hurt to have the FBI owe you one, so I agreed you could work on this project half time for the next five working days."

"Thanks, Marge, I appreciate it." Even though this task required more work for her it also gave her the opportunity to feel the excitement of pitting her skills against hackers. Something she enjoyed. Providing a level of satisfaction her normal work routine did not.

Marge's brows knitted together. "Do you really think there's more to the terrorists' plot than what you've already discovered? Will you need to check on the other two computers as well?"

Lucinda didn't want to say too much on the off chance a potential traitor in their midst overheard their conversation. "It's possible. I'll look, but I doubt I'll find much evidence. Yes, I believe I'll need to check all of them. Did the FBI bring the others?"

Obvious relief showed on Marge's face. "Then go ahead and start. Remember, *half* of your work day is to be spent on this. Yes, there are two others. When you finish with this one let the techs know and they'll swap out this one with another until you're done."

"I understand the restrictions. Thanks."

Marge left with a click of her high heels on the laminate flooring in the corridor.

Now Lucinda had the first computer and instructions from her boss. She set about making a copy on a portable hard drive. While that process worked away, she finished the rest of her regular work.

Once the copy completed, she stored the portable hard drive in a small safe in her cubicle. Marge allowed her to work on their non-sensitive assignments from home at times; perhaps she'd grant permission for this.

As she drove home, she called Jason. "Bear, how sweet of you to ask me over for dinner. How did you know lasagna was my all-time favorite?"

"I didn't, but it sure is mine. What day is convenient for you?"

"Tomorrow night would be great. Around 7:30?" Lucinda admitted to herself the idea of having dinner with Jason alone sounded appealing. She'd seen him around the building, at the gym and in various meetings. She wasn't keen on the idea of dating coworkers so she'd never allowed herself to flirt. Funny how things sometimes worked out.

"Perfect. See you then."

Lucinda spent the hours allotted mapping out the sections of code containing abrupt stops. Tracing the connection between sections, if any, could give her some insight into the overall strategy. She planned to do some preliminary work tonight on the copy then work tomorrow on the real computer. By tomorrow she might have something to share with Jason. She wouldn't have the full scope of the project, but she hoped for some indication of which direction to look.

CHAPTER EIGHT

A grin spread across Jason's face when the theme music to the James Bond movies filled the space. Somehow making that song the ringtone for the throw-away phone he used to communicate with *Baby* seemed appropriate. When at work he kept the phone on vibrate in his pocket so no one would hear.

After their brief discussion he disconnected the call while pulling into his parking space at the apartment building. Good thing he'd already purchased the items needed for lasagna. He'd prepare the dish so a warmup tomorrow night after work would make the meal ready faster. Toss a salad and make some garlic bread and he'd be done in no time.

Whistling as he took the steps two at a time leading to his second floor apartment, he didn't notice the dark van parking in the guest area across from his place.

Jason pondered what he and Lucinda should do if they uncovered significant suspicious activity. Notifying the FBI seemed like the logical thing to do. However, he wasn't too sure about their contact, that Shawn fellow. He'd bragged about once dating Lucinda. In spite of that Shawn hadn't taken Lucinda's comments seriously. Did he truly believe they'd caught the terrorists? Or did he want everyone else to accept the notion? Could Lucinda and he trust Shawn to follow up on any new leads they developed? If not the FBI, then who should they contact? The local police would probably send them right back to the FBI. And Shawn would be suspicious of their reasons for not reporting to him. If he was one of the terrorists, it would not go well for himself and Lucinda.

Round and round the thoughts whirled through his brain as he prepared the lasagna. Finished with the task, he turned on the television. He'd drown out his thoughts before going to bed otherwise he'd never manage to fall asleep. At least that was his plan. At five a.m. he climbed out of bed and stood in the dark, staring out his living room window. It overlooked the parking lot so not much of a view. He'd tossed and turned most of the night trying not to think of his brother, Trent. He seemed to be the one person who it made sense to contact.

After Trent left the army last year he'd attended the police academy in Charleston. Before he'd graduated, the DEA approached him to join them in a sting operation as an undercover operative. Jason understood they didn't need the Drug Enforcement Agency for whatever this was he and Lucinda were uncovering, at least he didn't think so. Of course Trent might have a contact at the FBI. One they could trust. He might not like his brother much, but he knew he could trust him.

A few minutes before his alarm's scheduled buzz, he noticed a dark van pull into the guest parking across from his apartment. If someone in a carpool parked there, then why did they continue to sit in the van? Were they waiting for someone to come out of an apartment? He shook his head thinking he'd become way too paranoid.

His alarm sounded so he strode back to the bedroom to shut the constant buzzing off and head for the bathroom to shower and dress for the day.

After a quick breakfast of a frozen sausage biscuit heated in the microwave and coffee, he gathered his usual gear for work. As he walked toward his truck he noticed the dark van again. Still there. Without a doubt, something was wrong. The vehicle followed him out of the parking lot and all the way to Ft. Jackson. They turned shortly before entering the facility. More information to share with Lucinda over dinner.

He frowned as he thought about the van. Did Lucinda have a tail, too? Thoughts of any harm coming to her made him freeze. How could he prevent it? The only reason she'd become involved was because of his discovery. He'd never be able to live with himself if something happened to her.

She'd need to be extra careful coming to his place tonight. With that in mind he formed a message in his head so he could slip a note in her desk. Normally he would do the transfer after work, but he needed her to see the warning before she left. Checking his watch, he discovered confirmed he'd arrived early. If he hurried, he could put the missive in her desk drawer before anyone else walked in.

CHAPTER NINE

Lucinda skidded to a halt by her desk as she noticed the clock indicating she was fifteen minutes late. Damn. She hated being late to anything, especially work.

As she put away her purse in a locked drawer she detected the center drawer open about an inch. Concerned about possible theft she took inventory of her office supplies. Then she checked the envelope with the card where she and Jason agreed to leave messages. Sure enough a new message waited. What was so important he needed to tell her something before tonight?

The note read:

Baby,

I noticed someone seems to have taken great interest in me of late. Not sure they are one of our friends who hired the musicians or someone else. Thought you might want to meet me at Andrea's place before dinner.

Bear.

Andrea? Oh, wait, she's one of the women from the gym and lives in the same apartment complex as Jason. She'd had a pool party at their complex last summer. Now she understood. He wanted her to park on the other side of the complex in case someone followed her and saw them together. *Good thinking, Jason.*

"Hey, gorgeous, why the frown?" Shawn walked up to Lucinda's desk.

"Shawn, what a surprise to see you." Frozen, she wondered what to do with the note.

"What has you puzzled?" He indicated the paper in her hand as he leaned on her desk way closer to her than she liked.

Lucinda folded the message and set it on her desk as if the object was inconsequential. "The usual. More patches to the operating system." She noticed the moisture gather on her upper lip. Hopefully, Shawn would not.

"The corrections to make our computer systems more secure and recommended by the owner of the operating system? Never ends, does it?" He leaned over and ran his hand down her arm.

She tried not to show her revulsion, but couldn't help rolling her office chair a couple inches farther away from him. She forced her voice to sound light and friendly. "Nope. Allows me to stay employed. What brings you here?"

He leaned closer to her with a grin. "You. Have you had time to find anything on those terrorists' computers?"

Lucinda laughed, sounding forced to her ears. "I'm not that fast. Give me a few more days."

"Time is limited for this extra effort." He sounded annoyed at her lack of progress.

Lucinda crossed her legs under her desk and one foot bounced erratically. "Yes, I'm aware. I'm surprised you are so interested since you initially didn't think the research necessary."

"I still don't believe you'll find anything."

Did his voice sound more angry than annoyed?

"Jason Meyers did mention you two had talked and he wanted to have the code checked out. Since he overviews the accounting aspects of several multi-million dollar defense systems, I figured we should make him happy."

Was Shawn's concern more for what she might find or for the military projects? "It makes sense to me. Don't worry, you'll be my second call if I find something."

Shawn seemed startled. "Second? You aren't going to call Jason first, are you?"

She wondered at the comment. "Of course not. I'll go through the chain of command and talk to my boss first, then you."

"Yes, that's the right thing to do." He let out a deep breath as if he'd been afraid Jason would find out first.

Why did she have such an odd feeling about what Shawn really wanted? She had more questions than answers.

"I'll let you return to work." Shawn threw the comment over his shoulder as he stalked away from her desk.

Lucinda wondered at his real meaning. Intent on finishing her regular work first ,she turned around and dove into the latest patches.

Once the allotted time for regular work ended she didn't pause for lunch, but immediately delved into the terrorists' computer. Her concentration blocked out everything else going on around her. All of a sudden she realized a headache banged against her skull. She needed to eat. Coming out of her work trance she realized no one else occupied her floor. The clock showed seven o'clock. Wow! She'd better finish up and leave or she'd be late to dinner with Jason. Scurrying around to shut down the computers, store them in a secure location, and gather all her materials for her talk with Jason, she all but ran out of the building.

On her way she made a mental note to watch if anyone followed her. Glancing in her mirror as she left Ft. Jackson she spotted a white sedan pull behind her. With little traffic at this hour she managed to keep track of the vehicle. The car sped up and slowed down, but never passed her.

Watching her review mirror more than the road ahead, she ran into a residential trash can set curbside for morning pickup. The loud crunch startled her. "Damn." She put her car in park and watched as her shadow passed her. Her hands shook as she removed them from the steering wheel.

Trudging up to the house the owner came out to meet her.

"Must a been texting and driving," the homeowner accused.

"No. Not at all. Looking for a house number." Her response came out a bit more agitated than she'd meant.

"Harrumph. Let's take a look."

Lucinda turned on her headlights so they could see the damage better in the fading light.

"Good thing these are made out of plastic. If we had the old aluminum cans you'd probably have smashed it. Your car took the worst of it." The homeowner pointed to scratches on her front bumper.

"Serves me right." Relieved the incident didn't require a police report she walked back to her car door. "I'll be on my way if you don't object."

"Go ahead. Look where you're going." The homeowner stalked back to his house.

As she wound through the residential area her shadow returned a block later, but kept farther back. Good thing Jason warned her, otherwise she'd not have noticed.

She parked near Andrea's apartment. Hoping Andrea was at home, Lucinda took her time to gather her personal laptop she'd left in her car and meander to the door. She knocked and then spied the white sedan moving to park in a dark area by the dumpsters. Dusk would soon turn into night. Slipping over to Jason's without being seen would be easier once full darkness fell.

Andrea opened her door. "Lucinda, what a nice surprise. What brings you here?"

"Hey, Andrea, can I come in for a second?" Her voice sounded as shaky as her hands.

A puzzled look on Andrea's face appeared before she said, "Sure. Come on in."

As Lucinda stepped inside Andrea started picking up some things in her living room. Lucinda racked her brain for an excuse to be stopping by for a chat.

"Don't bother on my account. I wanted to, ah, ask if you, ah, wanted to join me on a 5K run next Saturday. It's for charity. For military children who have a parent deployed."

Andrea turned from her last minute cleanup to face Lucinda. "Next Saturday? Sorry, I won't be able to make that. I already have plans. Family coming in town."

Lucinda put her hand on the door knob. "I understand. I happened to be in the complex and decided to stop in and ask."

"Thanks for thinking about me." Andrea smiled, but Lucinda noticed an odd look in her eyes.

Opening the door Lucinda stepped out while she said, "I need to go. Have a good evening."

Lucinda knew Andrea had been too surprised to ask more questions. Thank goodness. There really was a 5K run next Saturday. It had been the first reason she could think of for knocking on her door. Good thing she'd worn dark clothing to work. But her blonde hair would shine like a beacon. She took off the decorative scarf around her neck and made a sort of turban to cover her hair. Also removing her jacket she stuffed the thing in her bag along with the laptop. At least the absence of the extra bulk would give her a different silhouette if anyone saw her. She hung to the shadows and tried to avoid the external lights on the property as she made a dash for Jason's apartment.

CHAPTER TEN

About fifteen minutes later she knocked on Jason's door. It swung open immediately. She stepped inside before he had time to say a word and shut the door.

"You must have been followed." Jason gave her a concerned look and put his hand on her arm.

"Yes. Good thing you gave me that heads up. I parked by Andrea's as you suggested. I even stopped to chat with her for a minute before coming over here. Hopefully, they didn't see me leave since I stayed but a minute or two." As she talked she took off the scarf from her head and draped the item around her neck.

Jason motioned for her to sit down on the sofa. "I admit the fact you were late had me worried. What kind of vehicle followed you?" He'd felt more than worried. Terrified for her safety seemed more like it.

She paused a moment as her brows knitted together. "A white sedan. Maybe a Camry."

He joined her on the couch. "I have a dark blue van monitoring my movements. The vehicle shadowed me from home to Ft. Jackson and back. Of course, they pulled off shortly before entering the gate. Which means they don't have access to the post. At least not routinely."

"I noticed the car pulled behind me as I left post. Since I didn't leave until seven that made a tail easier to spot. I have no idea if they followed me to work, but after your comment I suspect they did. I wonder if other vehicles are waiting for us at the other gates? I routinely use the same one. How do they know that?" Lucinda paused and sniffed the air. "Sorry to switch topics, but I'm starving. I have a headache that won't quit until I have some food. By the way, that lasagna smells fabulous. Do I also detect garlic toast?"

Jason immediately stood up and motioned Lucinda to follow him. "Of course. Everything is ready. Have a seat and we can dig in."

"You're a lifesaver. I'd been concentrating so much on work I didn't emerge until way after my usual quitting time. Then I almost panicked when I realized I'd be late." Lucinda looked as if she melted into the dining chair.

He kept his expression neutral. "No problem. I understand. The need to keep them from connecting us is important. But I'd appreciate a text or something if you run late again." Downplaying his concern seemed the right way to speak to Lucinda. What would she think if she knew his interest was more personal than work related?

"Of course, I didn't think." She looked chagrined at her oversight.

Her safety had him concerned. Should he continue to involve her? If not, who else could he trust? Jason took the lasagna and garlic toast out of the oven. He'd kept the dishes warm waiting for her. Everything else sat on the table.

Lucinda's stomach growled.

He gave her a one-sided grin. "You weren't kidding, you sound hungry."

Spots of color appeared on her cheeks. "Sorry, I skipped lunch. I ate breakfast a really long time ago."

"Then I expect you to eat a big helping." Jason put an enormous amount of lasagna on each of the two plates.

"I think I will." Lucinda surveyed the offering.

"What do you want to drink? I have wine, water, iced tea, or soda."

"Although the wine sounds great I think I need to keep my wits about me so I'll stick with iced tea."

Jason filled two glasses and sat down across from Lucinda. She fidgeted while she waited for him to sit. She must really be starving.

"Dig in." He motioned to the food. "We'll talk when you feel better."

Before the words were out of his mouth she took a forkful of the cheesy pasta saying a quick, "Thanks," before shoving the giant bite in her mouth. Jason watched for her reaction. Her eyes lit up as the flavors sprang to life on her tongue.

"Wow. This is really fantastic. You're a great cook." She stuffed another big bite in her mouth and then reached for a slice of Italian bread that had been doused in butter and garlic then toasted to perfection.

"You can thank my mom. It's her recipe. When I was a teenager she made sure I knew how to cook."

"I'd be delighted to tell her sometime." She mumbled around the food in her mouth. "Does she live here in Columbia?" Lucinda continued to shovel food between words.

"No. That was a rhetorical comment. She died right after I graduated from high school."

He saw her stop in mid-chew then swallowed. "Oh. I'm sorry. I didn't realize."

"No need. You had no way of knowing. Speaking of family, what about you? Do you have any living around here?" He preferred not to talk about his family. Not that he had anyone other than his brother still living.

Lucinda's face changed. Her eyes lowered. "No family anywhere."

"Oh. Sorry." *Way to go, Meyers. Now you've made her sad. Shut up and let her do the talking.*

"Like you said, no way you'd know." After those few remarks they ate in silence.

Lucinda wiped her mouth with her napkin and lay it on the table. "Thanks for dinner. The lasagna was fantastic." Her words rushed out of her mouth as she continued. "We need to talk about the people following us and what to do next." Lucinda stood and took her plate to the sink. "We can talk while we wash the dishes, then I'll show you what I've found so far on the computers."

Jason followed her to the sink, his dishes in tow. "There's no need for you to help clean up, I'll take care of everything. Go sit down. You found something already?"

Lucinda motioned with her right hand. "I want to discuss these people following us before I tell you about that." She sat back down at the kitchen table while Jason finished putting the kitchen to rights.

"They must be the real terrorists. The ones who orchestrated those college kids into helping them." Saying it out loud made him more worried about Lucinda's safety. How could he protect her? He was a good shot with a pistol. Although he had a carry permit for his handgun it was illegal to transport it on Federal property where they worked. Perhaps he could have a personal trainer at the gym give him some tips for personal safety. Ones he hadn't already figured out for himself.

"Agreed. They know about me because I went in with the FBI on the sting. What about you. Why do they know about you?" Lucinda's forehead puckered.

Jason put his palms up and shrugged. "I'm assuming they know about me because I'm the one who monitors the financial portion of the weapon systems they targeted."

Lucinda tilted her head. "How would they know?"

After a significant pause, he frowned. "That's a really good question." He finally understood her real question. "I think they either have inside information or somehow have captured my credentials when I log into the system. Either way the scenario is bad."

Lucinda slowly nodded as if considering the possibility. "I can help with the potential captured credentials. I'll have one of our security techs stop by and scan your computer to make sure there isn't some kind of malware on your machine that captures keystrokes or anything else. I'll tell him you've been selected at random. We do that weekly so I'll add your name to the list."

Relieved she had at least one solution, he said, "Great. That will help us narrow down the possibilities."

Jason put the dishes in the dishwasher then they moved to the living room where Lucinda opened up her laptop and connected a portable hard drive.

"Exactly. I'll receive a report once he's finished. I routinely send out comments to the people who've had their computers scanned so an email from me won't be suspicious if anyone is checking."

Startled at the comment, he asked, "Are there ways for people to check emails sent back and forth between us?"

"Unfortunately, yes. Most people would find it difficult in our system and a limited number of people have legitimate access, but that type of tracking can be done."

"Can you check out the people who have access?"

Before answering his question, she said, "What's your wi-fi password?"

He anticipated that requirement and had it written down for her. Once he handed her the piece of paper with the information on it and she entered it into her laptop, she continued their conversation as if nothing had transpired. "I'll start looking tomorrow. Not sure if what I find will help. Most of the people are in the same department as mine, so if one of them is sharing the info, then figuring out who could be difficult."

"At least we'd have a list to review."

"Exactly."

He settled on to the couch next to her. "Good. We have a place to start." Her scent and closeness made him want to put his arm around her. Not now. She'd probably punch him and storm out the door. Stick to business. He kept his expression and tone neutral. "Now tell me about these *musician friends* of yours and what they told you."

CHAPTER ELEVEN

"As I'm sure you guessed the musician friends are hackers. Some people I used to hang out with online." Lucinda hurried on to keep Jason from asking questions she didn't want to answer. "One of them told me about another hacker I don't know. Supposedly, this unknown person was invited via the dark web to do some work for big money. He or she didn't accept and then ranted on one of the chat boards about suspecting a trap set by the FBI to take him/her down. The timing is right for those college kids being targeted."

"Did you reach out to this unknown person for more information?"

"I did, but haven't checked since last night to see if I have a response." Lucinda clicked several keys. "I'll look right now. There might not be one since we don't know each other. Especially since this hacker seems a little paranoid. All that stuff about traps from the FBI has no doubt made him extra careful." She gave a little chuckle and looked at him. "Of course, in this case the FBI did take them down although not for the reason this person suspected."

Lucinda could feel Jason's eyes on her as she read her messages, ones coming from the email address she used when she too had been a hacker. Her real life email account was kept separate so none of her former hacker friends would know about her current work. There would not be a good outcome for anyone if her former colleagues found out she worked for the government.

"Yes, there is something from him," she announced moments later as she turned her laptop for Jason to view.

After they both read the post, Jason said, "Yeah, he's careful all right. How do you plan to respond?"

"I don't want this to drag on forever." She paused as she considered some options. After inspiration struck, she said, "I'm going to appeal to his ego and ask for help for my poor cousin, Percy, who was arrested by the FBI."

Jason grinned. "I like it."

Her fingers flew across the keyboard creating a draft message.

"What do you think of this?" Lucinda showed him the message. She couldn't help the smile on her face.

I'm sure you asked around about me. You know I was an active hacker until a few years ago. I don't do that stuff anymore and don't know people involved now so I hope you can help me. My cousin, Percy, also became a hacker. He's been arrested by the FBI. I'm trying to find the people who hired him to do the job that ended in his arrest. Through the grapevine I heard you were also contacted. Do you know who they were or have an email address?

"It could work," Jason agreed.

She noticed the dimple in his right cheek as he smiled at her. That smile sidetracked her thoughts for a moment. Lucinda sent the note. "It could take a while for a response."

"Then it's a good time to have dessert." Jason stood and walked back to the kitchen.

Lucinda remained on the couch, but called out to Jason. "You made something for dessert, too?" She'd never had a man cook for her before. Somehow this seemed intimate even though the project was work related.

She took a moment to really look around his living room. Very masculine. Brown leather couch, a leather recliner, big TV, rustic coffee table, and not much else. One modern print hung on the wall that brought the only color in the room.

Jason laughed as Lucinda heard other noises coming from the kitchen.

She rose and walked to the bar to watch him. She admired the tight fit of his jeans and snug T-shirt stretched across his impressive chest and shoulders. His movements told her he'd been an athlete at some point in his life. She'd bet on swimming. Thoughts of touching his bare chest made heat gather in the pit of her stomach.

"No, I didn't make dessert. I stopped by the bakery on the way home. Hope you like cheesecake."

Taking a moment to register the reason for his answer, she snapped out of her momentary trance. "Who doesn't? I don't suppose you have some type of topping? Maybe some strawberries?" She couldn't help the pleading in her voice. Thoughts of food now seemed much more important.

Jason looked across the bar separating the kitchen from the living room. "No strawberries, but I have some caramel sauce. Will that do?"

Lucinda grinned and put her hand on her chest. "Be still my heart! Caramel is my absolute favorite." Good. Keep it light and simple.

"I'm beginning to think you say that about all food." Jason cut a slice for each of them and drizzled on the sauce.

"I suppose I do like to eat." She shot him a grin. "A lot."

Jason brought their dessert to the couch, setting their plates on the coffee table. "So what's your secret to not weighing three hundred pounds?"

Lucinda once again sat down next to him, enjoying his warmth and vitality. "High metabolism. And I work out at the gym. I've seen you there, too." Lucinda took a bite. "Ohhh. This is absolute heaven. You'll have to tell me which bakery sells this."

At that moment Lucinda's laptop dinged indicating a new email had arrived in her inbox. "I hope that is a response from our hacker." She set her partially eaten cheesecake on the table and checked.

"Yes. It's him." She hurriedly opened the message.

"I can't believe it. Look at this." Lucinda moved the screen toward Jason so he could read the message.

Your cousin should have been more careful. I knew they were setting up whoever agreed to the job. I don't have a name, but I did track their IP address. I keep a list in case they reach out again. I'm sure you know what to do with it.

Lucinda grinned. "Well, that's good news."

"You can find the physical address with it, right?"

"Yes. The location at the time they sent the message. If we're lucky it will be a house number. If not, maybe a coffee shop they still frequent."

Jason's eyes showed his excitement. "We can stake out the place and see if one of those cars following us turns up."

Lucinda held up a hand to slow him down. "Let's figure out the next step once we have something." Again she went to work, this time tracing the information. Her cheesecake sat untouched on the coffee table. Several minutes passed before success.

"Got it." She shot Jason a quick grin. "Now let's see if it's a house, apartment, or business." More clicking of the keys. "A business. It is a sandwich and coffee shop." Her shoulders slumped. "This means we don't have their actual address yet. We have to hope they will return to this same place."

"Then let's figure out when they were there and see if they show up on the same time of day and day of the week."

Liking his idea, she continued with the thought. "Now I have the IP address I can check for messages on the confiscated computer. If there is one, there will be a time and date stamp. It's worth a shot. Plus, if we can spot the car and copy down a license plate number we can find out who they are." Lucinda rolled her eyes. "Of course, we'd have to call Shawn for that information."

Lucinda picked up her cheesecake and started eating again.

"Not necessarily," he replied slowly as he seemed to consider the option.

She stopped before putting another forkful in her mouth. "What do you mean?" Her eyebrows shot up. "You want me to hack the DMV records?" She took a bite and chewed while waiting for his reply.

Jason furrowed his brow as he made chopping motions with his hand. "No, that's not what I meant. I could call my brother. He could find out for us."

Surprised, Lucinda said, "Your brother? I didn't realize you had one. Is he in the FBI?"

"No, a Charleston Cop. He went undercover for the DEA on his first assignment."

Impressed, she responded, "Really? I doubt the DEA is involved. Unless they used the money to buy drugs. That would be a whole other problem. What have we gotten ourselves into?" It all came out in a rush as the situation suddenly seemed so overwhelming Lucinda wondered if they were doing the right thing.

"Like you said earlier, one step at a time. We need to find out the date and time and see if one of these cars shows up at the place. I can take on that task. You're doing more than enough with all this computer sleuthing. I don't want you to be injured."

Her spine stiffened at the insult. "I can handle myself."

"I'm sure you can."

She could tell by the look in his eyes he didn't mean it. *Stop being so prickly*, she admonished herself. *He's being protective. At least I think that's what's going on. Since this is a first for me, how do I know?*

"I'm tired," she admitted. "We'll talk more when we find out something." All of a sudden Lucinda felt so weary she didn't know if she could drive the few blocks back to her place. She put her empty plate back on the coffee table. "I need to head back home and grab several hours of sleep before I do anything else." Lucinda rose from the couch to prepare to leave.

Jason glanced at his watch. "I didn't realize the time." He stood and helped Lucinda gather her things. "I'll walk you back toward Andrea's building. It wouldn't be wise to take you all the way to your car."

"Agreed. We don't want our followers to know we're in touch."

Jason's expression showed his concern. "I'll hang back in the shadows and make sure you arrive at your car without any problems."

"Thanks. I'll feel better knowing you're there." Lucinda could take care of herself better than most women. Her army training included self-defense classes. However, she didn't want to tangle with those terrorists alone with another option available.

"Right. Now, let's head over to Andrea's."

As they walked, Lucinda said, "I almost forgot. A thought about a couple new words for our code."

"Oh, really? You think we need them?" he said, in a teasing tone.

Once again that dimple appeared and almost derailed her thoughts.

"Don't be a smart ass. You were right. We need a couple words to keep our notes understandable. Let's call the terrorists Talent Scouts. As we've already talked about the hackers as musicians. Then the location they may be working from could be a home base."

He nodded his approval. "Sounds like you've been thinking about all this. So what do we call the place that might be their target?"

"I did a little considering. The target could be their venue."

They arrived at the mailboxes. "OK. I need to stop here. Call me when you make it to your apartment."

Lucinda smiled at the comment. She rarely had anyone care enough to make a statement like that. "Sure. I'll slip a note in the usual place whenever I nail down the time and date when they used that IP address."

"I'll be waiting. Thanks again for not thinking I'm nuts."

She gave him a wink. "Not at all. You made sense of what I couldn't figure out in the computer code. We'll shut these people down."

CHAPTER TWELVE

Stopping at the kiosk-like building housing the mailboxes wouldn't seem out of place if someone noticed him and he could watch Lucinda climb into her vehicle. Moments after she left, a white car pulled out. He stiffened at the thought of her in danger. Should he try to follow the follower? No. He had to be sensible. At this time they were only watching, not doing anything. As Lucinda thought, the white car was a Camry. He'd be on the lookout for it. Too bad none of the street lights shone bright enough to view the license plate.

Lucinda's idea that there could be more cars waiting at the various gates exiting Ft. Jackson gave him an idea. He'd leave via a different gate tomorrow and see if anyone followed him. How would they know? Did they have a tracking device on his car? He'd check tomorrow while at work and the followers wouldn't see him. Was someone in their office giving them a heads up?

Jason meandered back to his place. They worked well together. He'd been worried she wouldn't take his concerns seriously. Not only did she take his opinion as probable, but it seemed to validate her own concerns during the review of the confiscated computers.

Pleased he made a good impression with his culinary talent, he pondered what he'd make the next time they needed to have a meeting. He felt the grin spread across his face as inspiration struck. *You couldn't go wrong with pot roast.*

Jason finished cleaning up the kitchen then headed to his bedroom. The throw-away phone rang. It had to be Lucinda.

Not bothering to wait for a hello, she said, "It's me. I'm home. Thanks again for the fabulous meal."

Smiling at her rushed words, Jason replied, "Glad you enjoyed it. My mother would be proud."

Lucinda chuckled. "I'm sure she would. Sorry, I can't talk. I need to hit the sack."

"Of course, I'll talk to you later."

After Jason disconnected the call, he looked at the phone for a long time. The evening had almost felt like a real date. With a stunning beauty. When this cyber threat ended he'd ask her on a real date. One where he picked her up to go out to a restaurant or movie or both where they'd be seen by everyone. No more sneaking around. Yeah. He'd do that.

During the night he dreamt of Lucinda. They were outside in the dark. She strode about ten feet ahead of him. He kept calling her name, but she wouldn't stop or turn around. When he walked faster, so would she. Their fast-paced walk switched to a jog and then a run. People shouted at them. What were they saying? Shots rang out. Lucinda jerked to a stop. She fell forward. A pool of red ooze coated the back of her blonde hair. He knelt beside her then realized the red pool was blood.

He sat up in bed, sweating, the sheets tangled around his legs.

What the hell?

Climbing out of bed he walked to the bathroom to splash water on his face.

It had seemed too real.

He checked the clock. 2:00 am. Maybe a glass of milk would calm him down. So he sat on the couch drinking and thinking. What did the dream mean? Was Lucinda in danger? Simply a figment of his overactive imagination? He realized he'd never go back to sleep if he entertained more thoughts like those.

Remembering the method his high school counselor taught him, he emptied his mind to relax and sleep and concentrate on breathing. Back then he'd had trouble thinking too much about his mother and her imminent demise. Many a sleepless night were spent until he learned how to clear his mind. Actually, he never completely emptied it. How could anyone ponder nothing? Eventually he managed to contemplate one thing. Something wonderful, so as not to reflect on negative stuff; bad things, like what his life would be like after his mother died. Instead he set about mentally packing a duffel bag. He'd plan a trip to some far away location and prepare for that trip. Back then he'd put together things for his brother, Trent, too. They'd go together and have a great time hiking, fishing, hunting, all the things they'd done when their father still lived. Times he considered the best in his life.

Maybe tonight he'd throw some stuff in a suitcase for him and Lucinda. They'd go someplace fun like the Bahamas. Not a lot of clothing for Lucinda. Some itty-bitty bikinis and not much else. He felt a grin spread across his face when he pictured her in them.

Crap. Those thoughts took him to a place he didn't need to think about tonight either. Some parts of his body liked the mental pictures a little too much.

He rose and went to the kitchen to rinse out his glass before heading back to bed. As he settled into bed again, he decided he'd think of a trip without Lucinda. Where he'd hike, fish, and hunt. That should help.

Finally, he managed to sleep a few hours before the alarm exploded with buzzing and hard rock music. Stumbling to the bathroom, he showered and dressed for the day.

As usual the blue van followed him to the main gate of Ft. Jackson. The one he always used when traveling to and from work. He thought about whether they sat there all day waiting for him to leave work or if they showed up a few minutes before his usual departure time of 5:00 pm. Probably the latter. Otherwise the gate guards would notice even though they parked in a nearby business parking lot. Which meant he could leave during the day and they'd never know. That brightened his outlook. It meant he could stake out the sandwich shop when Lucinda discovered the time frame they frequented the place. As long as it wasn't on the weekend. Umm. That could put a kink in his plans. He'd need to learn how to shake the tail without them realizing he knew about them. Well, like he told Lucinda last night, one thing at a time.

CHAPTER THIRTEEN

Lucinda felt refreshed after her night's sleep. She jumped into work when she arrived at the office. It took a lot of discipline to perform her regular work and ignore the confiscated computers which is what she itched to work on. After amending the list for routine scanning, she sent it to the techs to perform. The list now included Jason's computer. She was anxious to find out if any kind of malware had been loaded on his computer as it could tell them so much if it did.

With that accomplished, she did a quick search from her personal laptop to find out more about the IP address she'd received last night. It took a couple of hours to hunt down some dates and times they used it at the sandwich shop. She jotted the information on a piece of paper. She'd slip it into Jason's desk tonight after most people left for the day. Being the lead security specialist for keeping desk top computers used by several departments updated with the latest software allowed her access to pinpoint locations of computers and their users. It would also allow her access without concern from other employees. She didn't want any more people to witness her visit than necessary.

A few hours later one of the techs arrived at her desk out of breath. "I knew you'd want the information right away, Lucinda." He slapped down a sheet of paper on her desk, panting as if he'd been running.

After a quick scan Lucinda acknowledged him. "Darn right I do. Which malware?"

The tech went into detail about the specifics.

The frown on Lucinda's face deepened. "This is not typical. You don't accidently download this variety from clicking on an attachment to an email or crazy ad on the internet."

"Exactly. It's what makes this so upsetting." The tech's hands were waving and slashing during their discussion.

"Did you discover the installation date?"

The tech's hands flew up in the air. "According to the time/date stamps, four weeks ago."

Lucinda didn't say her thoughts out loud. The timing put the setup a couple of days prior to discovering the initial penetration into the weapon systems. There was no doubt in her mind it linked to the terrorists.

"I'm assuming you made copies before removing it."

"Of course." The tech agreed. "We followed protocol."

"We need to set up a specific scan for all the other desktops to make sure no others have this same malware. Evaluate all the budget people first." Could more than one of their systems have been hacked?

"We knew you'd want to. Preparations are already in the works. I'll establish those priorities. Let us know when you have the go-ahead from the higher ups."

Lucinda contacted her supervisor about the malware which meant work on the confiscated computers remained on the back burner while they dealt with this new threat.

"Overtime is granted for everyone on your team until we have all computers analyzed and fixed. Start immediately," Lucinda's supervisor, Marge, explained after a quick conference call with the chief information officer.

Lucinda didn't hesitate deploying all the techs to this immediate threat. She pitched in to ensure a quick completion of the job.

How many other weapon systems had been attacked? They'd soon find out. Lucinda would personally look for the code fragments she'd found from the penetration into Jason's systems. Her gut told her those fragments were important. Even if that didn't turn up any additional traces she had other ideas to ensure the safety of their weapon systems.

As instructed by her boss, Lucinda joined Marge when she called the FBI.

"Shawn, this is Marge at Ft. Jackson. I have you on speaker phone. Lucinda Edwards is here in the office as well."

"What can I do for you ladies?" His voice sounded wary to Lucinda.

"We need to report finding more malware capable of performing penetrations to our systems. Unfortunately, the machines responsible are internal to our network and are directly related to the previous find."

A significant pause occurred before Shawn replied. "Are you sure?"

Lucinda and Marge looked at each other, both with raised eyebrows.

Lucinda answered, "Yes, we are sure."

Did Lucinda hear him sigh before responding? "Very well. I'll notify the technicians to come secure the machine."

"We set aside one of the machines for your inspection. The others have already been wiped although we did make copies for you. I'm sure you will want to have your techs verify everything and possibly do another search."

"More than one machine?"

"Yes. Several machines in our budget office were infected with malware. We're in the process of identifying whether more weapon systems have been penetrated."

"This is very serious," Shawn replied.

Did Lucinda detect a note of irritation in his voice?

"Indeed it is." Marge continued with detailed information about what they'd found and what they'd done to correct the problem as well as the testing currently going on to check all their weapon systems.

Lucinda filled him in on specifics when asked. She wondered about his initial response. He seemed more resigned than surprised. Could he be involved somehow? An FBI agent? She would run her suspicions by Jason. Maybe they could work it out together.

CHAPTER FOURTEEN

Jason wanted to speak to Lucinda about the malware she'd found. He knew her whole department worked on cleaning the multitude of computers from his budget area that had been infected. He would have to be satisfied with waiting until he heard through regular channels or the next time the two of them could speak.

In an effort to keep from dwelling on things he couldn't control he decided to head over to the local watering hole. He left via a different gate. Sure enough the blue van followed him. How could that be possible? Then he remembered he'd joined a group of coworkers and they talked about meeting up after work. Was one of them passing on information?

"Good to see you, Jason. What's up with you?"

Unfortunately he couldn't share the major events in his life. "Not much, how about you?"

"Dealing with my wife." The man shook his head and let out a deep sigh. "She's watched too much HGTV and wants to do a DIY project at the house."

"Whoa. That means time and money." Jason responded with sympathy. He had difficulty focusing on the conversation as he tried to figure out how the followers knew which gate he'd depart from.

"It sure does. We've been watching YouTube Videos on how to install hardwood floors. Suppose to be able to finish our living room in one weekend." He snorted at the comment. "Now all I have to do is find someone with a truck willing to swap with my Mustang so I can pick up the supplies."

"That sounds like a challenge. Good luck," Jason replied.

Other people joined them and the conversation switched to the baseball game currently on television.

Perhaps the followers had somehow installed an app on his phone to track him. If so, then why follow him? Maybe they wanted to see who he spoke to outside work. Possible. He'd ask Lucinda.

The next morning Jason took a note from his desk, it held an address with dates and times. He knew what it meant. This was where the terrorists had sent the inquiry out on the dark web to hire hackers.

He felt certain the people following them didn't watch during the day while he and Lucinda worked. After asking his boss for permission to take a few hours personal time, he rushed out to his truck then keyed in the address into his GPS. Leaving his phone at his desk just in case there was a tracking app on it. No one followed him. Good. When he arrived at the location he cruised by as if looking for a parking spot at the sandwich and coffee shop frequented by coworkers.

Not wanting to take a chance of being spotted by the people tailing him, assuming they were the ones involved, he drove to a parking garage a few blocks away. He took out a University of South Carolina baseball cap and sunglasses then walked to a clothing store across the street from the coffee shop. He looked for the van and Camry, but didn't see either. Most of the clothes near the window happened to be women's.

"Are you searching for a present for your wife?" asked a clerk.

Startled by the unexpected interruption Jason stumbled for a reply. "Wife? No. Um. Girlfriend."

Smiling, the clerk gave him the once over. "How nice. Do you know what size she wears?"

Panic stricken, he didn't have a clue what to say. "No. She's tall. Around six feet. Thin. About your size, maybe." His thoughts went to Lucinda.

"Then she'd wear an eight." Walking to a rack near the center of the store she asked, "What interests you? A dress, pants, sweater?"

Jason gazed back toward the window then at the clerk. "I'm not sure. Something nice. In blue."

The clerk glanced up. "Blue? Is that her favorite color?"

"Her eyes. The color of her eyes." He tried to act in an offhanded manner.

"Ah, I see." The clerk grinned and searched through the various garments then picked out some blue items.

He continued watching the window and spotted a van like the one that followed him. Damn! The same man he'd seen at the bar when Bob announced his impending fatherhood stepped out. Could the woman who'd met him there be his accomplice?

The clerk cleared her throat to draw his attention. "Would one of these items work?" She held out a couple of the garments.

"I need to think about it. Thanks for helping." Jason couldn't leave fast enough. He wanted to take a picture of the license tag and maybe the man if it could be accomplished without being seen.

Sauntering down the block across from the café he didn't cross over until he'd past the entrance. Parallel parked cars lined both sides of the street so he approached them from the back, snapping a picture of the van's license tag. He held the burner phone, pretending to check messages. Clicking pictures as he walked, he noticed a woman crossing the street. He stopped abruptly and entered the first store he came to. A pet shop. A bell tinkled to alert the staff of the entrance of a customer.

Appearing from a back room a young lady said, "Hello. Welcome. How can we help you today?"

Spouting the first thing that came to mind, he said, "A dog toy. My girlfriend has a dog and I want to bring it a surprise."

Smiling, the clerk said, "Wise man. Make friends with her dog and she'll love you even more."

"Right. That's what I'm hoping." At least this wouldn't cost as much as a dress, Jason thought. Who did he know who owned a dog?

Selecting something quickly he paid then strolled closer to the café. Not planning to go inside he once again had his phone at the ready to snap a picture if needed. With luck on his side, he spotted the couple leaving the cafe. The man faced the wrong direction, but he'd be able to obtain a face shot of the woman. Taking a couple more pictures he continued down the sidewalk. As he crossed the street he noticed a white Camry. Not sure if it belonged to the woman, but he decided to take a picture of the license tag just in case. She'd entered the café from this direction so it could be the one.

To avoid being noticed he strode back to the parking garage.

Okay, now I have a picture of the woman and two license tags. What now? Trent. I need to ask for help from

Trent to find out who these people are. I can't believe the first time in four years I speak to him I'll be asking for a favor. Damn. Maybe Lucinda will have a better idea.

When he walked into the building at work it occurred to him that he and Lucinda might take some time off once she finished with the current crisis. He could contact his brother and set up a meeting at their place in Georgetown. They wouldn't have to worry about being seen together or anyone listening to their conversations due to the remoteness of the trailer. A stranger would be spotted in a second. Of course, he'd try to make sure they weren't followed.

Renting a car would leave a trail for the trackers. How could he switch cars with someone without revealing the real reason? And keep the followers from connecting him to Trent? As a cop, anyone would be suspicious even if they learned Trent was his brother.

Trying to concentrate on his actual work seemed dull after his afternoon's adventure. He took a moment to pen a note to Lucinda. Although he suspected she'd be working overtime, he'd arrive early tomorrow to slip it into her desk.

Baby,

I took some pictures of a talent scout at their home base. When you're finished with your current project maybe we can take a day or two to visit an agent. No telling what advice he can provide us about the scout. Give me a heads up and I'll make arrangements for the meeting.

Bear

CHAPTER FIFTEEN

The analysis of all desktops took two long days, and the results were disturbing. Only the computers in the budget department had been infected. Not all of them, but several. The reason they'd discovered the breach was Jason's recognition of the siphoned money. Which led to the sting the first time, now this extra effort.

Lucinda and her team worked sixteen-hour days trying to correct the problem and ensure no similar ones occurred. New procedures were now in place to scan for breaches from the inside. A much more difficult task than external ones.

Wednesday night she walked to her boss's office. "Hey, Marge. It's done. Finally."

"Oh, Lucinda, what great news. I have a video conference with the FBI for our daily SITREP. You can do the honors tonight."

"A situation report? Sure. What time?"

"In about five minutes. Have a seat. You look beat."

"I am. However, I'm pleased with our accomplishments."

The phone rang and she filled in the team of FBI agents with all their finds and new procedures.

At the end of the call Shawn spoke up. "Thank you, ladies, for everything. Sounds like you've given us some new ideas for our own procedures."

"I'll prepare a document you can share with all other agencies. I'd hate for anyone else to experience what we did," Marge explained.

"Of course. Good night."

Lucinda had two more things to ask Marge. "As you know I made copies of the confiscated computers on a portable hard drive. I hope you will sign the paperwork for me to take the hard drive home so I can work on it from there. I'm convinced there is important information on it and I don't know if the agreed upon week to locate something is sufficient. I feel strongly enough about it that I want to work on it on my own time."

"I appreciate your concern and enthusiasm. Since none of the code is considered confidential, I'll sign it."

"After all this overtime, would you allow me to have Friday off?"

Marge laughed. "So you can work on the code?"

Lucinda only responded with a shrug and a sheepish grin.

"You deserve it. Since you'll be here tomorrow you can bring everyone up to speed then delegate the writing of all the reports and new procedures. Once you have that under control you're welcome to take a break."

Although Lucinda still itched to work on the confiscated computers she also wanted to find out what Jason planned for the visit to the agent. It had taken her a while to figure out he must be talking about his brother. So did he plan to travel to Charleston? She understood why he didn't want to make inquires on the phone or on the internet. They'd both become paranoid about possible detection.

Before leaving she wrote a short note for Jason so he could request leave for Friday as well.

Bear,

My latest project is a wrap. Friday will be a welcome day off. Do you still want to visit that agent? If so, I'm available.

Baby

She dropped off the note and strolled out to her car feeling tired, but satisfied about her accomplishments. Jason and she had a lot to talk about. Shawn hit number one on her list. Jason would know if there were grounds for concern. The follow-on question was what to do about it.

Once she arrived home, she checked inside her refrigerator. Not much to look at. She hadn't been to the store in over a week. Never one to cook much, she bought easy to prepare foods, fruit, and some yogurt. Out of fruit and yogurt, she took stock of the freezer compartment. One frozen dinner left. Oh, well, she'd be gone over the weekend so it would serve for tonight and she'd go to the store upon her return.

As she nuked the pasta dish, the garlic and tomato sauce aroma made her think longingly of Jason's lasagna. Her stomach growled. She laughed as she wondered if it was in appreciation of the meal about to be consumed or a complaint.

The more she thought about Shawn's possible role in the breach, the more convinced she became of his role of infecting the budget department's computers. To verify, she'd need some information from Jason. The installation of the malware had to be done with a flash drive directly to each machine. Jason would know if Shawn had the opportunity. Lucinda didn't want to ask anyone else in case her queries made their way back to Shawn.

What could his motive be? Money? Disgruntled with the government? She had no idea, but it didn't really matter. They'd have to dig deeper to prove any of her theories.

CHAPTER SIXTEEN

Jason read Lucinda's note Thursday morning. Great. They could take three days in Georgetown if needed. The office wasn't extremely busy right now so his request for leave should be granted. His enthusiasm wavered when acknowledging the call to his brother had become his first priority. Thinking about what to say took over his thoughts for hours.

Once his leave request was approved he contacted the coworker who needed to borrow a truck. Switching cars would keep their followers from tracking them.

At lunch time he grabbed the throw-away phone on his way to the truck to call his brother. He didn't want to chance their conversation being overheard.

After three rings a recording asked the caller to leave a message. Probably because Trent didn't recognize the phone number. Fine. It would be easier to leave a message than speak in person.

"Hey, man, it's me. I know you don't recognize the number, but please don't call me back at work or the other number. Just this one. I'm having a work problem and need your help. My other numbers might be tapped. Could we meet at the old house Friday night or Saturday? I'm bringing a friend and we need some help from someone we can trust. I'm sitting in my truck waiting on your reply. I'll stay here for thirty minutes. If you don't call by then, call me after five-thirty tonight."

Jason snatched the sandwich out of his lunch bag then started munching on it and the chips he'd brought. About fifteen minutes later the phone rang. He recognized the number.

He took a deep breath before answering. "Hey, man, thanks for calling back so quickly."

"How could I not? It's the first time you've called me in four years. And with such melodrama. Not like you." Trent's familiar teasing tone flowed through the line.

"Yeah, tell me about it. Like I said. I don't want to say much on the phone. Not even each other's names."

"Whoa! That serious?" Trent's tone changed.

"Seems like it. I'll explain all this weekend. Do you think you can take time off?" He tapped the steering wheel nervously waiting for his brother's reply.

"I'm not scheduled to work this weekend so I can meet you at the old place around eight tomorrow night. Will that be all right?"

He let out a breath he didn't realize he'd been holding. "Absolutely. Be sure to keep an eye out for any vehicles that don't belong. I'll be driving a red Mustang."

"A new car?"

"No. A loaner. See you tomorrow. And, thanks." Jason added the last bit although it was difficult.

"Of course, you're my little brother." Trent's response seemed genuine as well as surprised.

At that they disconnected.

He didn't understand his confused feelings. He felt grateful to his brother for helping with the situation, but also anger. Angry about how Trent left him with their dying mother so many years ago. In spite of the anger, he trusted his brother. Their parents always taught them to believe in one another, emphasizing the importance of a blood bond. *Not now,* he cautioned himself. Now was not the time to start soul-searching. Be grateful and sort it out later.

Thinking about spending a weekend with Lucinda made his concerns about his brother seem inconsequential. He decided to concentrate on the positive aspects of the weekend instead of the negative. Although it would be a working weekend they'd be able to spend some quality time together. The idea of showing her his hometown made him smile. He'd worry about his brother when they met face to face.

One more call to make. He decided to wait until after work. No telling if Lucinda could talk safely now.

Jason finished his lunch and wandered back into the office.

He and his coworker would do the vehicle switch at work the next morning. That way the man could have the truck all weekend. If the shadows followed the pickup after work, they'd be surprised to find someone else at the wheel. Leaving his regular phone at work should also throw them off the scent. He grinned at the chaos it would cause. The best part was they wouldn't realize he'd done the swap on purpose. At least he hoped not.

Once at home he made the call to Lucinda.

"Hey Baby. Those Talent Scouts might want us to audition this weekend. Pack a few outfits for at least three costume changes. Also, leave your other phone at work. I'll explain why later. If they call I'll pick you up by the cafeteria door at the usual time. We'll swing by your place to pick up your gear before going over." He figured she'd understand to pack for three days, but not bring her suitcase to the office.

"Will do. Yes, I understand. Not the cafeteria door though, how about the one near the gym?"

"That'll work."

"See you then."

CHAPTER SEVENTEEN

As instructed Lucinda packed for a three-day stay then left her large backpack next to the front door of her apartment. She took her computer bag when she left at her usual time for work, immediately spotting the white Camry following her. She drove to a fast food place and grabbed some sandwiches at the drive-through. As always her shadow stopped before entering Ft. Jackson.

She parked near the door to her office and sat in her car for a few minutes. Strolling slowly to the door near the gym, she kept an eye on the time. It wouldn't do them any good to have people notice her hanging around. About a minute after her arrival by the door, a red Mustang pulled up with Jason in the driver's seat. She dashed out, hopping into the car before he sped away the moment the door closed.

"Whew. I didn't notice anyone I know watch our departure." Lucinda looked over her shoulder.

"Me, either. The next hurdle is to exit Ft. Jackson without picking up a tail. I doubt anyone is watching, but you never know. Nervous?" Jason glanced at her as she crouched down in her seat.

Giving him a strained smile, she said, "A little. Not sure if I should hide my face or act normal. How come you told me to leave my other phone at the office? "

"Maybe pretend to look in your purse for something and obscure your face as we pass the gate. I put on my sunglasses and cap in case there is a camera set up as we exit the post. I'll look down like I'm fiddling with the radio."

"Sounds reasonable."

"I left the office the other day driving a different route. The blue van still followed me. I wondered how they'd figured out how to find me. So I thought someone may have installed a tracking app on my phone. The next day I left my phone at work during lunch time and went somewhere. No tail. Is that possible?"

They both did their hiding act as they left Ft. Jackson and for a few blocks beyond.

Lucinda's brows furrowed. "Yes, although I don't understand why they still follow us if they have a tracking app."

"I wondered that, too. Perhaps to see who we are meeting?"

Lucinda's eyes grew large. "Oh, yes, that makes sense. I'm glad you realized before this trip. Otherwise they would have been able to follow."

They both remained silent for a while considering the ramifications.

Jason broke the silence. "So far so good. I don't see the van or the Camry." He took off his cap and placed it on the seat behind him. He motioned to one of the cups. "I brought coffee. That's yours."

"Thanks. I noticed the heavenly smell when I sat down." She rummaged in her bag that contained her laptop and other essentials. "Here, I brought bacon, egg, and cheese biscuits." She offered him a paper-wrapped item. "I'm guessing we'll need to stop at your apartment as well as mine to pick up your bag, too."

"Yes. Mine is closest so I'll drive there first. I'll take the biscuit after I stow my backpack. It's just inside the door so I'll pull up and leave the car running. When you see me close the door, pop the trunk open." He pointed to the trunk release button. "I don't want to stay any longer than necessary. You never know who might be watching."

"Sure thing."

They remained silent while they stopped at each apartment then put their backpacks in the trunk. Munching on their breakfast and sipping coffee, they both relaxed as the distance grew.

"Whew. Even though I didn't think our shadows waited at the gate all day I couldn't help being anxious." Lucinda fluttered her hand. *Since when do I make silly gestures like that? Must be my nerves.*

"So was I. I'd been considering options for a couple days and tried to come up with a good way to handle this. The problem will be when we return. I'm sure our places will be watched. We can't afford to let them know we are working together."

Lucinda looked at Jason. "True. We'll think of something over the weekend. Maybe your brother will have an idea." She noticed he grimaced when she mentioned his brother. "How come you avoid talking about him? The first time you mentioned him and now you looked like you drank some sour milk or something as disgusting."

Jason's jaw clenched. "Long story."

Not giving him an opportunity to ignore her request, she replied, "We have a couple of hours before we arrive in Charleston, so go ahead."

"Charleston?" Jason took a quick look at her then back to the road. "Oh, sorry, I should have explained. We're not going to Charleston."

Lucinda sat up a little straighter in the car. "Why not? I thought that's where your brother lived."

"It is. But we're meeting at our old house in Georgetown."

The time difference to drive there wouldn't be much, so she shrugged and said, "Oh. Well, that's fine too. Why Georgetown?"

"If anyone knows as much about me as I think they do then I don't want to be obvious and drive to his house."

Jason's frown clued her in on the concern he felt for his brother. "You don't believe they'll expect you to travel to Georgetown?"

"Not at all. I haven't been there in over two years."

"Really? Why not?"

Jason sighed. "You aren't planning to let this go, are you?" He gave her a resigned look.

She grinned back at him. "Absolutely not. So you might as well spill the beans."

Starting with a deep breath, the explanation began. "I mentioned my mother had cancer, right?"

"Yes, you did."

"The diagnosis came late during Trent's sophomore year. He quit football and picked up odd jobs. He drove her to chemo when she became too sick to drive herself. Being two years younger, I took care of stuff at home like laundry and cleaning. That's when I learned how to cook."

Lucinda remained silent while Jason seemed to gather himself before continuing.

"At Christmas before he graduated from high school he and Mom started having arguments. They'd both ignore me when I tried to find out what they discussed. A few weeks before school ended, they finally told me. He joined the army and left about a week before graduation. He received permission from school to take exams early and they sent him his diploma later."

"So he didn't share the experience of the graduation ceremony with his classmates?"

"No. And he didn't tell any of his classmates at school. They all asked me what happened and I had to play dumb. He didn't want people to know." She heard the confusion in his voice.

"Why not?"

"Good question," he replied with a snap. "You'll need to ask him." He gave her a small smile when he realized his response came out too terse. "After her initial treatments, Mom went into remission for a while. The cancer returned after he left. By my senior year she was too sick to work and drew unemployment for a while then disability. We managed, but it wasn't easy. Since I did most of the chores I didn't have time to work. Most days I drove her to appointments and such along with school.

"That's when I really started to learn how to cook. She'd explain everything and I'd follow her instructions." He perked up when sharing the experience that he obviously enjoyed. "Then I started trying things on my own to tempt her to eat. In turn, she nagged me about attending college. No way could I leave her so I compromised and applied to Horry-Georgetown Technical College. The close proximity would allow me to live at home. She insisted I also apply to the University of South Carolina."

Again, Lucinda let the silence grow between them while he struggled to continue his story.

"She threw me a graduation party." He smiled at what she thought must be a good memory. "I don't know how she did it. A lot of help from friends, but even then it must have taken all her energy. I hadn't seen her so happy in a long time. Then a week later she died."

Her heart broke for him. "Oh, Jason, I'm so sorry."

"Me too," he responded in a small sad voice. After clearing his throat he continued. "That's when Trent came home. He was stationed in Afghanistan so it took a couple of days of travel for him to arrive. One of our neighbors, Mr. Harper, helped me with the arrangements. Apparently Mom had talked to him about it. She'd tried to tell me, but I refused to listen. She even pinned a note to the dress she wanted to wear."

"Oh, Jason." Lucinda couldn't think of anything else to say.

He looked at her with a sad smile. "Sorry, I didn't mean to upset you."

It took a few moments to bring her emotions under control. "What did Trent do?"

"He stayed four weeks. We cleaned out her closet and took care of the insurance, bills, and her will. Not much to it, of course. The house and land belongs to both of us. Then he went back to Afghanistan. I found a part-time job and spent the first year at Horry-Georgetown Technical College. He came home the next summer, but he'd changed. That's when I decided to transfer to the University of South Carolina." During the telling of this final portion of the tale, Jason's voice became hard.

"Yes, I know a lot of people who've been to the war in the Middle East. It changes everyone." She realized her comment didn't ease his anger. "So Trent decided to stay in the army?"

"Apparently. For a while longer. He ended up in the Middle East three times. He would call on occasions like my birthday and holidays." He sighed before continuing. "I didn't expect much when he was in a war zone. But I didn't think he would re-up after the initial four-year obligation. That would have been two years after Mother's death. I believed he'd come back home. Maybe attend college at USC with me."

She recognized the hurt in his tone. After a short pause, Lucinda asked in a soft voice, "Did you ask him why he didn't?"

"No," he said with a huff. "Figured it wasn't my business. His life."

Lucinda heard the sorrow in Jason's voice. "And you're mad at him for not coming home?"

He shrugged as if it didn't matter. "We don't have any other relatives. Guess he didn't care enough to return so I decided to leave him alone. I wouldn't have called him this week except I know I can trust him in spite of everything. And we need someone in law enforcement to help us."

"When did you two talk last?"

He glanced at Lucinda. "He's called a few times since he left the army last May."

She smirked at him. "Let me guess, you didn't answer the phone."

Shrugging his shoulder, he said, "Why should I?"

With a click of her tongue she responded with irritation. "Because he's your brother."

"He doesn't seem to think that's a big deal."

Releasing a deep breath and throwing up her hands, she said, "I'm not going to try to talk you into or out of anything. Maybe this weekend you can ask him the reason for all he did. His answers might surprise you."

"Umph. We have a lot of other things to discuss in the next couple of days. I doubt we'll have time for ancient history. Let me tell you about the Talent Scouts."

Lucinda knew this wasn't the time to prod him more into doing something he didn't want to do. She did vow to herself when the opportunity arose this weekend—and she was sure it would—she'd convince him to talk things over with his brother. Thinking about how much desire she had for a sibling, or any family member, his attitude made her unhappy. Not wanting to make them both sadder, she decided to allow the change of subject.

She dug into her bag again and pulled out a bag of M&M peanuts. She opened it and offered him some. "How did you figure out who they are?"

CHAPTER EIGHTEEN

"**W**hile you were busy fixing all the problems with the latest hack I did some sleuthing." Jason accepted a handful of the candy.

"Such as?" She crunched the chocolatey goodness.

"I went to the coffee shop you identified. That's where I found them." Jason felt very proud of his discovery.

Gulping down the sweet stuff, she asked, "How did you know who they were?"

"Remember the first time I came to your apartment with my crazy theory?" He glanced at her.

"Of course." She rolled her eyes.

"After work that same day, I stopped in at the local watering hole for a beer. I was so paranoid I thought this one guy watched me. Then a while later a woman joined him so I dismissed it as my imagination."

Lucinda's eyebrows were drawn together. "And they were at the coffee shop?"

"Exactly. I spotted him as he pulled up in a blue van like the one that's been following me. A few minutes later the same woman walked down the sidewalk and went into the same place. It couldn't be a coincidence."

"Did you see her get out of the Camry?"

"No, so I'm not one-hundred-percent sure it's the right car," he admitted. "However, it was parked in the right area where it could be hers. I didn't want to hang around to watch them leave. I felt I'd already pushed my luck."

"Sounds like it," she agreed. "Did you take their pictures, too?"

"I didn't have the right angle to take the man's picture, but I took one of the woman."

She grinned and held out the bag of M&Ms again. "Great job. I'm sure your brother can look up the license tags. Do you think he has someone to ask about facial recognition software for the woman's picture?"

Surprised at the request, he shrugged as he popped more candy in his mouth. "I have no idea, but I plan to ask. Of course, they were both Asian. I wonder if they are from

China or North Korea if the databases they use would recognize them."

"If they are in the country legally they should. What about the man?"

"What about him?"

"You said you saw him at the bar after work. Do you think someone might have taken a selfie with him in the background and posted it on social media?"

Jason's eyebrows rose at the idea, then he looked at Lucinda. "That's a great question. Someone might have." He paused a moment to think about what had been happening that evening. "Bob from work along with several other coworkers were there, too. Bob told everyone about his upcoming fatherhood. Someone might have snapped a shot with the guy in the background."

Lucinda clapped her hands causing a few M&Ms to spill out of the bag and on to the floorboard. "Good. Good. Since you have the date and approximate time I can troll social media and see what I can find with that geotag."

Jason made a mental note to clean up the spill before they were stepped on and chocolate stains messed up the borrowed vehicle.

He switched back to their conversation. "Geotag? You mean you can search Facebook with the location information from pictures people post?" He shook his head at the thought. "Thank God you know how to do stuff like that. I wouldn't have any idea how."

"Some people turn off geotagging on their photos, but most don't," she pointed out. "So I can only find the pictures with it. Besides, that's why you came to me in the first place, remember?"

Her expression of joy made his heart flip. "Yep. It was the smartest thing I've done in a long time." Sure she would assume the comment dealt with their search for answers, he smiled.

Lucinda returned his grin at the compliment then her expression became serious. "I have another question for you."

"Shoot."

"Around the time you discovered the first hack, did you see Shawn hanging around your office?"

Jason frowned. "The FBI agent Shawn?"

"Yeah, him."

"I've seen him in the office before, but I can't say when," he admitted.

Tilting her head and wearing a puzzled expression, she asked, "You saw him before all the hacking stuff? Why would he be in your office area?"

"He knows a couple of the guys in my department," he explained. "They have lunch together a couple times a month. Sometimes they eat in the cafeteria, while other times they meet off campus."

"Hmm. That's interesting."

Confused by the change of subject, he said, "Why are you asking?"

"It's only a feeling. Nothing concrete." She waved a hand in dismissal.

Put out with her reluctance, he urged, "Tell me. We have to figure out who's behind this mess and what they're really up to."

"True." She paused only a moment. "So, when my team and I discovered your machine and several others had malware on them, we dug deeper. The only way that particular malware can be installed on a machine is by someone walking up to it and inserting a flash drive to download."

His head snapped around to look at her. "What? I thought you could acquire viruses and stuff by opening attachments from emails."

"You can. But not this type. It needed a more up-close installation." She hesitated. "It means we have a traitor in our midst."

His eyebrows rose. "And you suspect Shawn?"

Shaking her head slowly, she said, "Maybe. I've had a bad vibe from him since the first time we met."

"Didn't you date him?" It's a question he'd been dying to ask although he didn't want to act like a possessive jerk. Her remarks had opened the opportunity he couldn't pass up.

"A couple times while still in the army," she agreed. "I met him when I did some work for the FBI back then."

"Even then you wondered about him?"

"Not like if he was a traitor or anything," she quickly pointed out. "Something that made me think he isn't everything he says he is."

"Oh. I admit I never liked him," Jason said. "But didn't consider him a traitor."

"And I'm not saying he is," she clarified, "only that it is a possibility. When we notified him about our findings, his response seemed less than positive."

"What do you mean?"

"It's hard to describe." She continued after a moment. "But I'm not the only one. When my boss, Marge, and I talked to him on the phone we both looked at each other when he responded. You know how you do. When something doesn't sound right you look at the other person and you both have a surprised look and can tell they're thinking the same thing you are, like 'What the hell?'"

"Yeah, I get it," he said slowly. "Let me think about the date and I'll try to remember that far back. Unless something happened that day to make it stand out, I might not have made a mental note or even questioned seeing him."

"That's what has me worried more than anything else. If it's normal for him to be in your area, then anything he did would not seem unusual. A great way for someone to slip in something like malware. While you're thinking about it, try to remember if the majority of the office personnel were away from their desks at the same time. Like for a staff meeting or mandatory training. So many machines were infected he could have done them all at one time if the area was unsupervised."

"Sure, I'll think about it. I have my day planner with me. That should help me figure out if the office had a special meeting or something." Jason needed to make a list of everything he needed to do this weekend. The list kept growing.

"So what does Shawn have to do with the people following us?"

"They must be working together, don't you think?"

"You suppose Shawn hired them?"

"Or they work for the same people," Jason suggested.

They drove on in silence for several minutes before Lucinda asked, "You said you never liked Shawn. How come?"

"As you mentioned, difficult to explain. He seems phony to me. Always asking favors of the guys he hangs with."

"Like what?"

He squirmed in his seat before answering. "Small stuff. Sometimes he asks, can you give me the phone number of the hot chick down the hall? Or do you know where so-and-so goes on vacation? She always has a great tan." He took a quick peek to see if she understood what he was trying to explain. "Guy talk, but there always seemed to be an agenda for the questions. Not the obvious one, something I could never figure out."

"That does sound strange," she said with a puzzled look.

"I dismissed it as my annoyance because he seemed to marginalize women."

Her head tilted. "So the questions were always related to various women?"

His eyebrows rose. "Yeah, they were."

"Think more," she urged. "Who were these women? Were they in positions where they might have information he could use?"

"Good Lord." Jason realized she was right. "I suppose they were. Like you."

"What do you mean, like me?" Lucinda asked with a snap in her voice.

"Sorry, I guessed you knew." Now he'd made her mad. No, not him. Shawn.

"Knew what?" Her voice grew louder and more annoyed.

"He's always talking about you like the two of you were once a big item and he dropped you, but came to regret it and wanted you back. I thought he was bragging."

Lucinda sat up straight and clenched her fists. "That no good... Never mind." She paused as she appeared to grapple with her emotions. "I understand now. At least I think I do. Sounds like he trolled for information and thought he could use women to obtain it. I bet he used his so-called buddies, too. Having a few drinks and suggesting they talk about work."

"It's not like we have top secret information," Jason pointed out.

"No, I realize that. But keep in mind each of you has knowledge of sensitive information that when it is combined can become secret."

Jason nodded slowly. "True. We do work on the various weapon systems, the money side of things."

"And my bet is a lot of money is involved in whatever's happening," she pointed out.

"Yes. Enough that when hacked could provide funding for all types of terrorist activities." His eyes widened. "Holy Cow. I think we might have figured out who's behind all this. The Chinese or North Koreans."

Lucinda pondered his remark. "The Chinese do have a history of trying to penetrate U.S. government systems. Any system. This attack seems different, more specific. Nothing we can prove. Not yet, at least. He's working for someone. Someone who pays big bucks for the intel. Like a foreign government. Also, he can help slow down any investigation into what really has happened. This thing has become a lot more complicated."

"I hope Trent has a contact who can help us."

"It will have to be unofficial which will make it more difficult. If we plan to point the finger at a government agent or a foreign government we better have rock-solid proof."

Jason felt stunned at what they'd figured out. He looked at Lucinda and knew she must feel the same way. They sat in silence for the rest of the drive. Both contemplating the ramifications and how to prove it. Trent would be the key in uncovering evidence. Without his help the only way they'd find anything would be through Lucinda's hacking skills. Whatever she found would not be admissible in court, and it would also taint their integrity.

CHAPTER NINETEEN

Wanting to stop thinking about potential threats for a short time, Lucinda took in the sights of the small coastal town, Georgetown, as they drove through. She'd been here a couple of times with friends, but not with a person having the local knowledge Jason had.

"I know this town came into being long before we won our independence from Britain," Lucinda said.

Jason acknowledged the change in topic with his response. "The town itself was established in 1729. The Spanish landed here in 1526, although they never created a settlement."

"Indigo and rice were their big crops back then, right?"

He confirmed her statement. "Indigo first, then rice. Georgetown has a rice museum on Front Street."

"Yes, I've toured it during a previous visit." She remembered it being small, but interesting.

"Did you have lunch at Thomas Café?"

"I don't remember the name of the restaurant where we ate, but I don't believe it was Thomas."

"It's a couple of doors down from the museum. More of a local place. The original family who owned it sold it a few years ago after running it for eighty years or so."

"Really? That's interesting. Eighty years is a long time. Did it survive that really bad fire around 2013?" She envied his connection to this small town. Knowing so many people for such a long time. Them knowing you. What would that feel like?

"Yes. You read about the fire?"

"I did. How awful so many historical buildings went up in flames." Making a face, she couldn't keep from saying, "Oh, God. What is that horrible smell? I've smelled the same thing in Charleston."

Jason chuckled. "The paper mill. I agree it is awful. When you live here you become accustomed to it. Fortunately, it doesn't smell like this all the time. The wind has to be blowing from the right direction."

"Or the wrong direction. Ugh. Like rotten eggs or worse." She wrinkled her nose.

He laughed out loud at her antics. "What were we talking about before you went down that rabbit hole? Oh, yeah, the big fire. I didn't live here then, but I had friends who were affected. All of the buildings were businesses, but some had living quarters above. Fortunately, all but one has rebuilt."

They didn't drive down Front Street or the adjacent historical district which was the area Lucinda knew. Instead, they drove to a more rural area near a river.

They traveled a short distance down a dirt road. "Here we are. I have to admit I'm surprised the grass isn't taller."

"You mentioned you haven't been back in a while. Is Trent taking care of it?" She surveyed the tired-looking trailer. She admired the rose bushes near the front porch deck and flower beds on each side. The roses weren't in full bloom, only a few buds. Daffodils and tulips swayed in the gentle breeze. Happy colors of red and yellow made it look homey and welcoming.

"Given the shrubs are neat and the grass short, most likely."

"Do you have a key?"

"Yes. Unless Trent changed the locks. I'll check before we unload the bags."

He walked up a path lined with monkey grass then climbed the three steps to the front door. She saw him push the door open then turned to give her a thumbs up. He used the car key fob to pop the trunk open while walking back to the car.

They carried their booty into the house.

"Let's open a few windows, it's stuffy in here. Then I'll check out the rooms to make sure we don't have any unwanted guests."

Startled by the comment she looked around. "Guests?"

"Yeah, like a raccoon or something."

She relaxed after the explanation. "Oh, I see."

"Sorry, did you think someone from Columbia beat us here? Unlikely," Jason insisted. "I meant when you have a trailer this old that is raised above ground level, some animals think it's an invitation to take up residence."

She laughed at the idea. "I can't say I want to share a room with one."

"Exactly." Jason flung open some windows in the living room then went down a hall.

Lucinda grappled with the window over the kitchen sink and finally managed to open it. She decided to wait at the kitchen table before venturing forth with her luggage. Hearing Jason walk through other rooms and open windows, she noticed he took a while to return. She looked over the trailer, it seemed a typical layout. The front door opened directly into the living room which opened up to the right and toward the back. To the left of the door, the kitchen table stood where she sat in one of six chairs. Adjacent to the table there was a door leading to a hallway where she assumed the bedrooms and bathrooms were located. The other side of the hallway the outdated galley kitchen stood in its faded glory.

"Sorry it took so long. I couldn't help checking out the changes Trent's made to the place."

"Oh, sounds like you don't approve."

He waved a hand as if to negate her impression. "They're all right. Someone must be helping him."

"Why do you say that?"

"I don't think he would have chosen the paint color." She noted his odd look as if he were trying to decipher a code.

She grinned at his obvious displeasure. "Is it pink or something?"

"No. I don't know what you call it, but it's that color somewhere between blue and green."

"Aqua or teal?"

"Something like that." The concept seemed to be beyond his understanding. "I think only women know the names."

Lucinda couldn't help but laugh at his comment. "So you're saying Trent wouldn't have picked the color without help."

"Exactly. And I doubt he would bother with new bedspreads either."

"So it would seem there is a woman in his life."
Lucinda grinned.

"Must be. I wonder why they're fixing up this place."
He looked around as if the answer might be hiding here in
the living room. "He lives in Charleston."

"You both own this place, right?"

"Yeah. I don't know about Trent, but I couldn't bring
myself to sell it even though I doubt I'll ever live here."

His obvious attachment to the place tugged at her
heartstrings. "I can understand that. If I had a family home,
I'd want to keep it, too."

"I mean I wouldn't mind hauling the trailer off, but I
want to keep the land. Our folks bought this trailer as a
temporary place to live. They had plans to build a house on
this property. Then Dad died. After that Mom had her
hands full keeping up with the utilities and putting food on
the table."

"I know teenage boys put away a lot of groceries."
Lucinda hoped her joke would help lighten the mood. Talk
of his deceased parents had to be difficult so she helped
move the conversation to a happier subject. "So what
would you do with the property if money wasn't an issue?"

Lucinda believed this house and land had become the
representation of Jason's struggle with reconnecting with
his brother after the loss of their mother. Not only in a
physical way, but also an emotional one. Perhaps they

would find a way to come back together starting this weekend.

CHAPTER TWENTY

Jason cast his eyes at the ceiling. "Half the land is Trent's so it's something we have to decide together. After seeing the changes he's made, I suppose he wants to keep the trailer. We've never talked about it."

"Maybe you should."

"Yeah. Maybe. Why don't we give the house time to air out and we can grab a bite of lunch before settling down to business?"

"Sure. What time is Trent coming?"

"He said he'd be here about eight o'clock tonight."

Lucinda gathered her purse as they headed to the door. "Will he eat dinner before arriving or will we be waiting on him?"

"He didn't say, but that's pretty late. I'll send him a text so he knows to eat something before he comes in. I suppose we could have dessert and coffee when he shows up." He suggested it because he thought Lucinda would like the idea. Pleasing her seemed more important than worrying about whether Trent ate dinner or not.

"That sounds great. We can pick up some brownies."

Ah, yes. She did have a sweet tooth. "Or while you're doing your techie stuff, I can cook dinner for the two of us and make some brownies from scratch. I'll need to make a stop at the grocery store at some point."

Lucinda put her hand over her heart and turned to look at Jason before she opened the car door. "Be still my heart! I can't imagine having made-from-scratch brownies. You really know how to do that?"

He blinked several times in surprise. "Of course I do."

They climbed into the Mustang and drove to Front Street. "I think you should experience Thomas Café and its lunch options." He parked in front of an old brick building. A dark green canopy that covered the width of the café boasted the name in large, bold white script.

"Absolutely." She rubbed her hands together as she followed him to the door.

They entered the restaurant. He looked at it with new eyes, like Lucinda. Clean, but old. Several booths lined the walls with small tables placed in the center.

Before Jason had time to sit down, one of the waitresses squealed and gave him a hug. "Oh, my God,

Jason. It is so good to see you. Where is your brother? And who is this beautiful lady you brought with you today? Is she your wife?"

He liked the idea of Lucinda being his wife more than he wanted to admit, even to himself. "Slow down, Marcie. Give me a minute to answer your questions. Trent won't be here until later. I'll tell him to be sure to stop by this weekend. And this is a friend and coworker, Lucinda. No wife."

"Well, maybe she will be some day." Marcie gave them both a knowing look.

Lucinda smiled and shook hands with the gushing waitress. "If so, that is a long way down the road."

Jason felt heat creep from his neck to the top of his head. Lucinda looked at him and chuckled.

Marcie motioned Lucinda to a chair. "Sit down and let me bring you something to drink. Iced tea, lemonade, coffee? What do you want?"

"Unsweet iced tea for me. No lemon," Lucinda said.

"Unsweet tea? What kind of southerner are you?" Jason quipped. "Marcie, I'll have sweet tea with lemon."

The waitress left menus before she rushed to the back telling everyone Jason Meyers had returned for a visit.

"Guess you've been here a few times, huh?"

"That obvious?" he asked with a grin.

"I think it is pretty special that you've been gone all this time and people still remember you and greet you so warmly."

"Georgetown is not a big place. Everyone knows everyone else. Sometimes that's good and sometimes it's not." Remembering the times he or Trent had run into trouble, it seemed his mother knew about it before they made it back to the house.

"I wouldn't know. I've never lived in a place this small."

He didn't know how to reply to that comment. What was Lucinda's story? She knew all about him. At least more than most people. He'd make it is mission this weekend to discover more about her.

Turning to the menu, he said, "We better decide what we want to eat. She'll be back in a flash."

Lucinda perused the menu. "Oh, they have shrimp and grits. That's what I'll have." She slapped the menu down and gave him a smug smile. "Since I've moved to South Carolina I can't have it often enough. And look. They serve fried green tomatoes with it, too."

"And they are the best you'll ever eat," Jason said with a nod of approval.

Marcie set their drinks down and glanced at Jason. "I suppose you'll have your usual? The crab cake sandwich?"

Jason smiled with a nod of agreement. "You know me too well."

The waitress looked at Lucinda with her pen poised over the order pad. "How about you honey? What will you have?"

Lucinda chuckled during the brief exchange. "If I tell you, will I have to order the same thing every time I stop in?"

With a sly smile the waitress replied, "Of course not. Just keep in mind if you have the same thing at least three times in a row, we'll remember and assume that's what you want unless you tell us differently."

"Thanks for the warning." Lucinda handed Marcie the menu. "This time I'll have the shrimp and grits. So you know, I plan to try several other items on the menu."

"I'd be disappointed if you didn't," the waitress replied with a grin. She spun around and trotted to the back with the menus and order.

"So what do you want for dinner tonight?" Jason asked.

"What are my options?"

Boasting about his culinary expertise, he said, "If it's southern, I can make it, along with a few Italian and Mexican dishes."

She shrugged. "I don't know. What do you want?"

He pondered the question a moment before replying. "Maybe some pork chops?"

Lucinda's lips formed a perfect bow at his suggestion. "Sounds delicious. Are you going to make lasagna again sometime this weekend? I know it makes a big batch."

How could he possibly say no if she wanted some? He'd do anything to bring a smile to her lips. Those luscious lips. They mesmerized him. Realizing he needed to answer her, he said, "If that's what you want, sure. I can make it tomorrow night while Trent's here. If I remember right, it's one of his favorites, too. I'll check the pantry to see if there's anything in there before I go to the store. I doubt he comes here often enough to keep a lot."

An elderly couple who had been sitting a short distance away stopped at their table as they left. "Jason, we're so glad to see you. How have you been? Is your brother in town for the weekend, too?" Not giving him a chance to answer, the woman continued. "It's nice to see both of you boys back in Georgetown, even if it's just for a weekend." She patted his hand.

Jason introduced Lucinda to the couple before they departed, then an old classmate came by. "Hey, man. Good to see you. If you're in town long enough, stop by Fish Tails and we'll have a drink."

"Sorry, not this weekend. Maybe next time." He surprised himself by realizing he'd like to do exactly that.

"You bet. I know a lot of the guys would like to see you." The man waved while giving him a big grin.

Lucinda's eyes widened when Marcie sat the huge platter in front of her.

"Maybe we should have a salad for dinner. I'm not sure I can finish this and eat another big meal today," she said.

"I know I'll be hungry so I'm still putting pork chops on the list. However, I'll make you a salad if you like," Jason teased. If he knew anything about Lucinda by now, he knew she'd be hungry by dinner.

While they ate, another former classmate walked into the restaurant. "I heard you were here. I had to stop in to see for myself." A young woman gave Jason a big hug as she eyed Lucinda.

"Would you like to join us?" Jason asked after introducing Lucinda. Not that he really wanted her to, but the politeness his mother had instilled pushed him to make the offer.

"No, no. I only stopped by for a minute. I couldn't pass up the opportunity to see you. You look great. Come by daddy's store when you have a chance so we can catch up."

"Sure." He smiled as heat rose from his neck to the top of his head. Although the surprise comments pleased him, they also embarrassed him. He had no idea so many people cared about whether he returned to Georgetown or not.

They paid and left the restaurant after Jason hugged several of the waitresses and the owner who'd come from the kitchen.

As they walked out the door, an elderly woman started to enter. She stopped short when she spotted Jason. "Well, I'll be. Jason Meyers. How are you?" The woman gave him a big hug.

"Ms. Mackey. Good to see you. Still teaching English?"

"I retired last year. How about you? What are you doing now? Last I heard you graduated from USC."

"I did. Now I work as a Budget Analyst at Ft. Jackson." Jason was pleased he had a good report to give Ms. Mackey. She'd been a favorite teacher.

She patted his hand. "Well, now. That's good to hear. Always happy to find out what my former students are doing. And who is this lovely young lady?"

Jason grinned as he said, "Lucinda Edwards. I'm showing her my hometown."

"I'm pleased to meet you, Ms. Mackey." Lucinda accepted the woman's a hug.

"I can't believe how friendly everyone is," Lucinda said as they drove away.

Jason explained, "It's called Southern hospitality."

"Or maybe they think you're special," she said.

Once again he felt the heat rise from his neck to the top of his head. He'd lost count how many times over the last couple of hours she'd seen him do that. How embarrassing. Grown men didn't blush.

"Let's head back to the house. You need to start working your magic." Jason said.

She gave him a saucy look. "Right. It's time to settle down to business."

CHAPTER TWENTY-ONE

Jason set about making a grocery list for a pork chop dinner and a lasagna dinner as well as breakfast for a couple of days. Any leftovers they could take back to Columbia with them. He'd pick up one of those Styrofoam coolers. He left Lucinda to set up her computer on the kitchen table.

"I'm guessing you don't have wi-fi since no one lives here permanently." Lucinda typed away on the keys of her laptop.

"If we do, it's news to me." When Jason realized what that meant, he slapped his hand to his forehead. "Oh, shoot, I didn't think about that."

She waved away his worry. "That's okay. Most of my work will be done offline anyway. If I need it, I can always create a hot spot on my phone then connect through it."

Relief washed over him. "Like I've said before. Thank goodness you know how to do all that techie stuff. I sure don't."

Lucinda shrugged. "We simply have different skill sets, that's all."

"Right." He chuckled. "I'll finish up this list and head to the store. Is there anything special you'll want for breakfast?"

Not looking up from her task, she replied, "As long as there is coffee I don't care."

"We have coffee. I checked."

"Don't forget you promised made-from-scratch brownies. Be sure to put those ingredients on the list." Lucinda glanced up with a smile that almost blinded him.

Nearly overwhelmed by a sudden urge to kiss her, he paused and blinked at her while struggling to hold back his desire. The need to kiss her just about overtook his other thoughts. He gripped the edge of the counter to prevent himself from taking her into his arms. He swallowed the temptation. Too soon for him to act on his desires. "Of course. I wouldn't want to disappoint you, now would I?"

She chuckled as she dropped her gaze back to the screen.

Thank goodness she didn't seem to notice his momentary confusion. His attraction to her had been growing the more he learned about her. Not only beautiful, her confidence and skill made her so much more attractive. Yep, a total package.

Remembering his need to check his day planner, he strode to the bedroom where he'd stashed it. He flipped to the day in question.

He returned to the living room. "My planner wasn't much help. It says 'mandatory training'. I'll try to remember the specifics while I run to the store."

"Good idea. See you later." Once again she spoke without looking up.

Taking the list and the car keys, he ambled to the door. "If you think of anything else, give me a call on the burner phone."

"Sure, sure. Take whatever time you need," she mumbled.

Obviously, she'd already zoned into work mode.

On the way to the grocery store, he thought that afternoon might be a good time to find out more about her. Before Trent showed up. From some of her remarks he knew she didn't have a family. Something they had in common. So what was her story? He'd ask over dinner. Giving her a break from computer stuff could be helpful. After a change in subject that required deep concentration he always felt more focused.

With the date of the malware install in context, he concentrated on remembering everything he'd done and the people surrounding him.

He hadn't been in the store more than ten minutes before the same thing happened to him as when they'd been at the Thomas Café.

"Jason, I heard through the grapevine you were back in town. Staying long?" An old friend from high school asked.

"Just for the weekend. You still live here?"

"Yep. Working at my Dad's accounting firm. What are you up to?"

Before he responded, a couple of people from his old church joined them.

He looked at all of them so he only had to reply once. "Working at Ft. Jackson in the budget department."

"Hey, that's great," one of them said.

Another replied, "Wow, you sound like you're doing great."

A third chimed in, "Will you be coming to services on Sunday?"

"Sorry, not this time. Maybe next time I'm in town."

He had to admit it pleased him that so many people he'd known cared enough to stop by for a word. Perhaps he'd start returning a little more often to catch up with old friends. He savored the idea while he finished shopping and drove back to the trailer.

When he walked in the door, Lucinda didn't even notice his arrival. It would seem she had a gift for tuning out everything when she had a difficult task to perform. He'd need to remember that. If he left her alone again, he'd make sure he locked the door in case a not-so-friendly person decided to pay an unwelcome visit.

After putting the groceries away, he located the battery powered shop vac and went outside to clean up the spilled candy from the car. At least the heat wasn't so bad that the chocolate melted. Back inside he made the salad she'd requested then started in on the brownies. Once finished, he popped them in the oven.

All the while he thought about the day the virus had been installed. He did some prep work for the pork chops. Somehow he figured she might eat one after all the good smells coming from the kitchen. He fixed two for himself then turned to the side dishes. Mac-n-cheese and some fried green tomatoes. Now all he needed to do was actually cook the fare, he decided as he surveyed the lot.

"How long have you been back?" she asked.

Startling him out of his reverie, he flinched. "Hello to you, too."

She shot him a sheepish look. "Sorry. When I'm in the zone I don't notice anything going on around me."

"So I noticed." He walked over to the table then sat down.

"I tend to block out everything else," she said with a shrug.

"Good to know. I'll be sure to lock you inside next time I leave you alone."

She offhandedly responded, "Oh, yes, that might be a good idea." She sniffed the air like a blood hound. "Are the brownies done?"

He laughed. "I should have known that's what grabbed your attention."

She joined in the laughter. "Yes, they smell divine."

"You'll have to wait until Trent arrives." He shook his finger as he admonished her.

With a delightful pout she responded, "I know and it will be torture." She stood up and stretched.

Having difficulty not watching her breasts as her blouse tightened across them with her stretches, Jason broke the spell by asking, "Want to take a walk around the yard before you delve back into the land of ones and zeros? Or do you have something to report?"

"Still checking on things. By the time Trent arrives I should have something to share."

He walked back into the kitchen as he tossed a question at her. "Have you taken time to look for a picture of that guy from the Facebook posts?"

"I started a search that's been running in the background." She sat back down and started to type. "Let me take a look."

"Not right now. I'll take the brownies out of the oven then we can take a stroll. Make you walk out the kinks from sitting so long. After that you can check." He opened the oven door and used a pot holder to remove the chocolate goodies.

"Okay." She stood back up. "A little sunshine and fresh air sounds good."

They ambled down the front steps and on to the dirt road a ways then back to the house. Admiring the spring plantings and crisp air had reenergized him. He hoped it helped Lucinda as well.

Should he make his feelings known? No. If she didn't feel the same way then it would make working together more difficult. He'd better squash his feelings a little longer.

After they returned to the house Jason sauntered to the living room and motioned for Lucinda to join him on the couch. "I have something to share with you."

"Really?" She sat next to him and turned to look at him. "About what?"

"The day you think someone installed the malware on our computers."

Her eyebrows shot up and delight appeared on her features. "You remembered something?"

"The mandatory training I mentioned earlier turned out to be an active shooter drill. It gave me something to put the date in context. You're right. Shawn did stop by the office. The drill took most of the morning. When everyone returned, the usual group and Shawn walked over to the cafeteria for lunch. I met up with one of my buddies there and we sat a few tables away. They talked and laughed so loud it annoyed a lot of other diners."

"Ah, so now we have some proof." Her eyes shown with success.

"Not really, only knowledge he was in the vicinity," Jason pointed out. "Not that he did the deed."

"True." Lucinda frowned. "It does make it more plausible. When we tell your brother at least this gives our assumptions a more realistic probability."

"We'll need a lot more information before we can take it to the authorities," he warned.

"Agreed. We'll set that aside for now. Let me look at what my Facebook search uncovered."

Lucinda sat down and Jason pulled a chair next to her. Breathing in her scent made him close his eyes and enjoy the picture his imagination drew of the two of them kissing.

"Do any of the men in these photos look like our terrorist?" Lucinda asked, not taking her eyes from the monitor.

Thankfully, they were sitting side by side and she hadn't noticed his closed eyes. Jason focused on the photos scrolling by on her computer screen. "There, that's the woman. You can't see the man's face, but maybe in a few more pictures we'll see him." He concentrated more until all at once a full-length photo of the man came into view. "That's it. That's him. You were right. You did it. You found him." He rubbed his hands together.

"We found him." Lucinda corrected. "If you hadn't told me about stopping at the bar, I wouldn't have been able to narrow down the date, time, and location of where to look."

"Now we have pictures, license tag numbers for our terrorists, along with a theory about how the malware got uploaded." Jason rose from the chair and headed toward the kitchen. "I think we deserve to take a break and have some dinner."

Jason decided his new favorite music was the sound of Lucinda laughing like she did right then. She continued working on her computer while he started cooking dinner.

Before long he said, "Time to turn everything off and set the table. The food's almost ready."

"Yes, boss. Right away, boss." She chuckled then shut down everything and moved the equipment so they would have a place to eat.

"Hey, you don't get a free ride because you are working. This is work, too."

"I know, I know. Teasing you is too easy and too fun." She smiled. "Point me to the utensils Chef Jason."

"Now I like the sound of that." It was his turn to chuckle.

They worked in harmony as she set the table and he put the finishing touches on their dinner.

"I'm guessing you might have more of an appetite than you thought right after lunch. So I fixed you a pork chop as well as your salad."

"And more fried green tomatoes?" She rubbed her hands together as she checked out all the goodies he'd prepared.

"Yes, those too. I noticed you enjoyed them at the Thomas Café this morning."

"I do. Thanks for not listening to me. Although I can't eat like this every day." She patted her stomach, indicating it would swell with the extra calories. "Everything smells wonderful."

They sat down after Jason plated their food and brought it to the table.

Lucinda sighed as she took her first bite of the pork chop. "Oh, that is so crispy, juicy and tasty. I've never eaten a pork chop this good."

"Such compliments. Coming from someone who didn't intend to eat another bite after lunch, you sure are managing fine."

Smiling and chewing at the same time, Lucinda swallowed. "I know. It's a bad habit. What can I say?"

"Glad you're enjoying the meal. Seems like it's the least I can do when you're working so hard on tracking down the bad guys."

"Hey, all this started because of you alerting everyone to the discrepancy you located. You've also been the one to track them down in the physical world."

Jason demurred. "Somehow it seems less important."

She set her utensils down and shook a finger at him. "Don't put yourself down like that. You have a significant role in all this, too."

"I don't want to talk about me anymore." Exactly the opening he'd been hoping for. "You learned all about me on the drive here. Now, it's your turn to spill."

CHAPTER TWENTY-TWO

Lucinda paused with a forkful of food halfway to her mouth. "Me? What do you want to know?" She finished inserting the delicious bite into her mouth.

"You mentioned you don't have any family. What's the story there?"

Chewing slowly, she took her time before responding. "Not much of one. I don't remember having a father. My first memories include my mother. Just the two of us. We lived in an apartment building in Atlanta. A lady in our building took care of me while my mother worked. Then one day Mom didn't come home."

"Lucinda, that's awful. What happened?" He had a look of horror on his face.

Keeping emotion out of her voice, she continued. "A car accident on her way to work."

"How old were you?"

"Six. Mom took me to school that day." Memories flooded back. "Before school let out, a social worker came with the neighbor lady to tell me what happened. Afterward, I went into foster care." Somehow the food had lost its appeal. She put her knife and fork down then placed her hands on the table.

Jason reached over and touched her hand. "I've heard some horror stories. Did you find a good family?"

Trying to be positive, she smiled. "At first, yes, I did. They were great. I called them Mom and Dad. About the time I turned twelve, Mom became pregnant."

Jason's eyes bugged out. "Then they gave you up?"

"Not initially. They'd been trying to adopt me. I guess they'd given up on having a child of their own." Lucinda took a moment before continuing. "Once I found out they were going to have a baby, I became angry and said a lot of ugly things."

"You didn't want another child in the house?"

"No, I didn't. I realize now it was about my insecurities. At the time I believed they wouldn't pay attention to me once they had a baby of their own. I had tantrums. As a last resort I threatened harm to myself and the new baby. To be fair to them, they did try to find help for me. I ignored everyone. In the end they didn't have a choice. They had to let me go before I did something awful."

"My God. That had to be as bad as losing your mother." Jason took her hand in his and gave it a squeeze.

Grateful for his concern, she squeezed his hand then released it. "True. I was angry for a long time. I spent the next six years in six different foster homes and six different schools. It's surprising I managed to graduate high school." The chuckle she tried to make came out a bit strangled.

"Is that why you joined the army?"

"Hmph. Not exactly. A tale for another day." Not many people knew the whole story. Thank goodness. "With no money for school or a way to support myself the army seemed the best option." Determined to make him see the positive aspects of her trials, she explained. "That decision worked out well for me for a number of reasons."

He cocked his head. "Why's that?"

"When you're in the army you automatically have a group of people who become like family. Sometimes even closer than family. I still keep in touch with a lot of them. It also helped me to think about something other than myself. A greater purpose, if you will."

Wanting him to understand where her passion for her work came from, she continued her explanation. "Before I joined I'd done some hacking so one of my mentors helped me channel those skills into a more positive goal. I took some night classes then when I completed my four- year commitment I had an associate degree. Once separated, I used the GI bill to take more classes then I ended up in the co-op program here at Ft. Jackson."

"So you went to school one semester and worked one semester until you finished?"

"That's the way it normally pans out. But I signed up for night classes while I worked so I finished in a year instead of two. I've been lucky."

"It doesn't sound like luck to me." He beamed at her. "You've earned everything you have and it couldn't have been easy. No one cheering you on or helping you over obstacles we all have as we become adults."

"By that time I had my army family. I still have them as well as a new set of friends here."

"Now I feel like a schmuck complaining about my brother," he said in a deprecating manner. "At least I have one."

"Exactly." Lucinda grabbed his hand. "That's why I want you to start communicating with him again."

"All right. I give." He threw his hands in the air. "How can I argue after what you told me?" Jason stood with his empty plate. "If you're finished, I'll take your plate so you can set up your computer again."

Happy her story helped him see reason, she smiled widely. "I'll assist with the dishes then check out a few more things before Trent arrives."

CHAPTER TWENTY-THREE

Eight o'clock on the nose, they heard a car pull up to the house. Jason walked to the front door. He barely opened it when Trent took a step inside then grabbed him in a bear hug. Jason stood stiff with no emotion on his face as his brother pounded him on the back.

In spite of his earlier promise, he held some resentment. After their mother died Trent had barely been in contact with him. He'd needed emotional support and Trent wasn't there for him. Isn't that what brothers were supposed to do?

Trent drew back with a huge grin on his face and ruffled Jason's hair like he had when they'd been young.

"Hey, it's good to see you. I almost drove to Columbia and hung out at your door until you showed yourself." Trent scanned Jason from head to toe. "You look good, kid."

Jason didn't know how to respond to that. "Thanks for meeting us here, Trent. I appreciate it." Trent seemed different than the last time he'd laid eyes on him. The haunted look no longer dominated his features. The three-inch scar on his right cheek had faded. Perhaps the memories connected with it had, too. The woman behind Trent seemed familiar. What was her name? "You brought someone with you?"

"Yes, yes, I did." Trent turned to the woman and grabbed her hand, pulling her farther into the room. "You remember Shelby. Shelby Cornwell. We're engaged," he said proudly.

Certain an expression of shock showed on his face, he could only repeat the word. "Engaged?"

The wide smile Trent had been wearing the whole time somehow grew even wider. "That's what I've been wanting to tell you with my phone calls. If you ever returned them you'd know that." He shook a finger at Jason.

"Congratulations." Knowing it would be expected of him, he stepped forward and gave Shelby a hug. They both appeared to be happy. He did want that for Trent. So how come he really wasn't?

Looking at the kitchen table, Trent noticed Lucinda. "So you have someone with you as well. Don't tell me, this is your girlfriend?" Trent went over to Lucinda and gave her a hug.

"No, no, we aren't …" Jason started explaining then was interrupted by Lucinda.

"Not dating. Coworkers. Hi, I'm Lucinda." She stepped back.

Apparently embarrassed, Trent said, "Sorry. Guess I jumped to conclusions."

In true Southern woman fashion, Shelby smoothed over the awkward moment with a glance at Jason. "The last time we saw each other must have been before your high school graduation."

Taking a moment to place her face and name, he finally said, "Right. You were in school with Trent? And your mom and mine were friends. I remember her stopping to visit Mom."

She'd been a shy girl back then with freckles and long hair pulled back in a rubber band. The short curly hair she wore now suited her new bubbly personality. Maybe her personality had changed due to the happiness the two of them shared.

"Trent and I were in the same class." She gave Trent a warm smile. "Our moms were friends. Mine still talks about what a wonderful person your mom was."

Jason didn't really know what to say so he murmured, "Thanks. She was a special lady." He cleared his throat. "Let's all have a seat at the kitchen table and I'll explain why I asked you to come here."

"Of course, of course." Trent pulled out a chair for Shelby then sat next to her. His eyes drilled into Jason. "You were so mysterious. Are you in some kind of trouble?"

"Maybe." He glanced at Lucinda with a worried look. "It's a long story. Let me fill you in on what we've discovered and some theories we have."

For the next several minutes, Jason and Lucinda explained everything that had happened in the last few weeks as well as their conclusions with the evidence and theories they'd developed.

"Man, this is a big mess," Trent said when they finished. "You don't really have any proof of anything. A lot of theory and assumptions. Which appear valid," he added when he seemed to notice the frown on Jason's face, "but nothing that would hold up in court."

"Exactly," Jason admitted. "That's why we need some help. Since our prime suspect is an FBI agent we didn't know who to tell or where to ask for help. I thought you might be able to help us find the proof we need."

"Of course I'll help. Is there something specific you wanted me to research? Sounds like the two of you have a really good handle on the situation."

Taking a slip of paper from a pile on the table, Jason handed it to Trent. "I have the license tag numbers of the cars that are following us as well as pictures of the two people. Can you find out their names and anything else that might help?"

"Sure, I can do that."

"Actually, I'm not positive the tag for the Camry belongs to the woman. If you can find out their names and their driver's license pictures maybe we can confirm."

"Once we have their names, I can run them through the terrorist watch list to see if they show up." Trent folded the paper and slipped it into his pocket.

"Somehow I doubt they will. We do need to find a connection between them and the FBI agent. Do you have any ideas on how?" Jason asked.

Trent frowned in concentration. "That could be a lot harder. Perhaps Shawn worked on a case they were involved in. I'm not privy to that type of information. Even if I was, I'd need a time frame or the type of crime involved to start the search."

Lucinda spoke up. "It's also possible the person who is orchestrating this is the connection between them. I believe the one way we'll find more answers is through the computer code."

"Give me a few minutes to check out these license tags then we can go from there." Trent pulled out his cell phone to log into the DMV database. "Damn, I forgot we don't have wi-fi here. Guess I'll need to drive into town." He ran his hands through his hair.

"No need." Lucinda took his phone. "I can create a hot spot on your phone then you can connect to the internet."

Trent's eyebrows shot up. "Thanks. That will make it a lot easier."

After a few clicks on his phone, she passed it back to Trent.

He took it and keyed in the information. "Okay, I have the registration information. Now I'll check for their driver's license." Again he typed more information into the phone. "Here they are. The man is Min Ro, the female Mee Pak. Do these photos match?" He passed the phone back to Lucinda.

Jason took out his phone and pulled up the pictures he'd taken at the coffee shop. He compared the photos with the ones Lucinda held. "These are the two people following us all right. Thanks, Trent. At least now we have their names."

"There's more than a name and address when you check a Driver's License. Give me a minute." Trent scrolled down and his eyebrows shot up. "Interesting stuff. Both these people are from South Korea. Here on student visas."

"I didn't realize foreign students with a visa could obtain a driver's license," Shelby said.

"Sure. They can even get a social security number since it is a requirement for anyone who works."

"Do we really think they are from South Korea? Their passports could be fake. I think it's more likely they are from North Korea or maybe even China if they are trying to steal money or technology," Lucinda commented.

"I doubt we'd be able to prove anything without involving the FBI or some other alphabet agency," Trent acknowledged. "I can do a background check, but I'll need to be at my station house in order to check secure databases."

"How about the DEA? Do you have some people there you could ask?" Jason queried.

"Before I do, we need to make a plan of action. I'm willing to reach out to them. However, let's talk about what exactly we're going to ask, when and what kind of information can I share or keep from them. This whole situation could transition from bad to worse if we aren't careful."

"I think we should keep as much information as possible from them. Give them only the basic details," Lucinda said.

Jason spoke up. "I agree. I feel comfortable telling them we suspect a federal agent of being complicit with a computer breach. Ask them what type of information we need to provide authorities to open an investigation. And who should we ask to open the investigation, their boss, or a regional agent in charge?"

"That's a good start." Trent wrote down the questions on a pad. "Think about what else you want to ask and I'll put it together in the morning before I call."

"While we're thinking, how about a brownie? Jason made them from scratch earlier today and I've waited long enough."

"I'm so glad you said that," Shelby said with a laugh. "I've been wondering if my imagination had been going into overdrive. I thought I smelled chocolate when we walked in the door."

"It's been driving me crazy since he made them." Lucinda echoed Shelby's laughter. "I'll pour the milk. Who else wants one? Or would anyone like coffee?"

"Milk sounds good to me." Trent pulled some glasses down from the cupboard.

Jason grinned for the first time since Trent walked in the door. "Sure, I'll take a glass. A little late for coffee for me."

Shelby found the brownies sitting on the counter next to the stove and cut them up while Trent pulled down some plates and opened the drawer to select some forks. They all performed their simple tasks then took the goodies back to the table.

After his first bite, Trent said, "Oh, man, that's really good. Tastes like Mom's brownies."

Appreciating the backhanded compliment, Jason said, "Of course they do. Who do you think taught me how to make them?"

"I don't suppose you also know her lasagna recipe? Trent's been talking to all the ladies at church trying to find someone who knows it," Shelby said in an offhanded manner.

"He does." Lucinda spoke up before Jason had a chance to answer. "I've had the pleasure of consuming a healthy portion."

Trent snapped his head around to look at Jason. "No way, man! You've had the secret all along? You have to give it up. I can't tell you how long I've been dreaming about it."

A sly smile emerged on Jason's lips. "As a matter of fact, I plan on making it for dinner tomorrow night. Do you want to help?"

Trent slapped Jason on the back. "You couldn't keep me away with a baseball bat. Hell, yes, I want to."

"All right then. We'll need to start about one o'clock. The sauce takes a while to make then simmer." He couldn't help his feeling of pride.

"Can I ask another favor?" Trent asked.

Jason shook his head and sighed as if the request was too much. "Sure. You need a kidney or something?"

Trent snorted. "Not that extreme. Do you mind if we invite Mr. Harper to join us? Anytime I come for a visit, I try to stop in and see him or ask him over for dinner."

Jason's eyebrows shot up. "That's a great idea. How's he doing?"

Mr. Harper had been there whenever Jason needed help with his mom. He'd always bring over fresh vegetables and fruit from his garden. A couple of times they even went on a hunt together. Jason's mouth watered when he remembered the venison steaks they'd shared. He smiled at the memories as he waited for his brother's reply.

"For a man of his age, he's doing fine. When I was undercover we visited several times. He seemed pretty down at the time. Lonely, I think. His daughter doesn't live in the area so he didn't have much company. That's changed now." He looked at his fiancée with pride and love. "With Shelby and her mom's help, the church sends someone around at least once a week if not more."

"That's good to hear," Jason said.

"Shelby, what kind of work do you do?" Lucinda wanted to include her in the conversation.

"I'm an event planner. I used to work in Myrtle Beach, but I managed to switch to a hotel in Charleston a few months ago." Her eyes looked in Trent's direction. "So I could be with Trent."

"That sounds like a fun job," Lucinda said.

"It is. It is also grueling work. You wouldn't believe what some people request," Shelby said as she rolled her eyes.

"I can only imagine."

Trent spoke up, "She's also a whiz at websites. You won't believe the incredible designs she's put together."

"Now that's a real talent. I can code all day long but designing an attractive web page is beyond my capabilities," Lucinda admitted. "I guess I don't have that much imagination."

Lucinda pulled out her computer. "Sorry to change subjects, but we need to get down to business. Let me explain what I found today."

"Is this one of the computers the FBI confiscated? I didn't think they'd let it out of their sight." Trent's expression showed he didn't approve if it was illegal.

Shelby quietly took the dishes away from the table to the kitchen.

"No, this is a copy of the files. The actual computer is back at my office. I'll be working on that next week. It should hold even more information."

"Really? Why aren't they the same?" Shelby asked with her brows knitted together.

"If anyone tried to delete information then the actual computer could still have trace information on it that can be restored. With a copy like this all you have are files not deleted."

"Oh, I had no idea," Shelby replied.

"Nothing is ever truly deleted. To wipe out all evidence, there are programs that will write over the entire drive multiple times then delete it. It obscures anything previously written in that sector of the computer. Since we were able to confiscate the machines before anything like that could happen, I should be able to recover some files they hoped to wipe."

Shelby walked back to the kitchen table. "Thanks for the explanation. I've heard people say nothing is ever deleted, but I didn't understand how it was possible. Your simple explanation makes it clear."

"So what did you find?" Jason prodded.

"I found a file containing some messages from the people who hired them."

"That's surprising," Trent said.

"Not to me. I figured these college kids were smart. They'd want proof someone else told them to do this in case things went bad."

"Which it did. So how come they put in those logic bombs to wipe everything when they need this file to prove someone else paid them?"

"I'm sure they have another copy somewhere. Probably on a flash drive. No doubt their lawyer has it and plans to use it for some concessions."

"So what do these messages say?" Trent asked.

"They have a code, kind of like the one Jason and I have been using. Nothing too difficult to break, but at the same time no words were used that would trigger an investigation. Words like bomb, hacking, malware or such. This first one is from the IP address we identified from Min Ro and Mee Pak who we believe are the terrorists."

"As agreed we have installed the instructions. Start your research. When you finish send us the entry points."

"I believe the word instructions means malware, research stands for hacking. The entry points must mean the college kids were supposed to send them a back door so the terrorists can gain access." Lucinda glanced from one to the other, her gaze finally landing on Jason.

Jason stood up so fast the chair he'd been sitting in crashed to the floor. "Good God! You mean there's been an undetected penetration into the weapon systems?"

Lucinda put a hand on his arm to calm him down. "Truthfully, I don't think they've done anything yet."

Jason paced the living room. "Why not? It sounds like that was the plan."

"I agree," Lucinda asserted as her right heel tapped against the aging linoleum floor. "With all the extra scans and scrutiny right now, any such penetration would have been detected. I think they are waiting until things calm down and we believe we've closed up any holes in our systems."

"You think this is a long play," Trent suggested as he rubbed a finger up and down the scar on his cheek. "They'll wait until no one is paying extra attention, then they'll make their move."

"Exactly. Because they've created a legitimate login and password while everyone's been checking out those college kids," Lucinda explained.

"These emails are the kind of proof you need. Since they used code words any decent lawyer will keep those people from going to jail. They may not even be charged," Trent acknowledged.

"I know," Lucinda agreed. "It's frustrating. I'm hoping the actual machines will give me more. After I return to work, I'll be able to bring it to my boss's attention. Once I do that, I believe she'll give me free rein to continue looking. Maybe even provide me some help."

Jason flopped back into his chair. "She'll have to report to the FBI, right? It'll tip off Shawn."

Lucinda nodded. "I've been considering that. Perhaps we can come up with an explanation so she doesn't. Then I can gather more information before we do. If the information is so damning, then Shawn may be forced to tell his superiors. Otherwise, they may think he has something to hide."

"He could bolt," Jason said.

"He might. Since we'll be watching, he won't make it very far," Lucinda said.

"Okay." Trent stood up from the table. "We have a good start. It's getting late. Why don't we all grab some sleep and start over in the morning? Fresh eyes and all that."

"You'll make the call to the DEA in the morning, right?" Jason asked.

"Absolutely. After we decide what questions to ask."

"Then we'll talk more in the morning. The coffee pot is ready. Whoever wakes up first needs to turn it on."

They all wandered down the hall to their respective rooms while turning out the lights as they went.

Jason laid in bed thinking about all the revelations today had brought. Lucinda had shared her early childhood memories. His brother was getting married to Shelby. They had names for the people following them. Lucinda discovered a coded message. Damn. No wonder he felt exhausted.

After more than an hour of restless tossing and turning, sleep finally claimed him as he anticipated another day of revelations. Would Trent's call to the DEA bring them closer to their goal?

CHAPTER TWENTY-FOUR

Jason heard Trent as he padded to the kitchen in bare feet. He'd always been the first one up in the morning. Knowing he would start the coffee brewing, Jason took a few moments to gather his thoughts for the day. *I don't understand Trent at all. He seemed so happy to see me. How come he's connecting after such a long time? Does he think I'll forgive and forget? Maybe it's Shelby. She was always nice to me and Mom; maybe she is pushing him. Lucinda and I do need his help. I suppose I'll owe him one for this.*

Jason sauntered into the kitchen to grab a cup of coffee before heading to the shower. Carrying his steaming mug, he turned down the hallway and almost ran into Lucinda. Her hair stood up in spikes, no makeup, and her eyes were barely open. She looked beautiful.

"Good morning, gorgeous." The words popped out before he had time to think. When he did, he was glad he'd said them. He meant the compliment.

Lucinda's eyes blinked at the comment. She obviously tried to determine if his comment was sarcastic or real. "Hey. Coffee."

He grinned at the way she said good morning. She'd warned him mornings didn't agree with her. Continuing down the hall, he grabbed some clothes from his room before heading to the bathroom for a shower. He heard voices coming from the master bedroom so he knew Shelby and Trent were also dressing for the day.

Minutes later Jason emerged from the bathroom and let Lucinda know it was vacant. After her coffee she seemed more alert and hurried past him to take her turn with the shower.

Once Lucinda emerged she joined the others at the kitchen table. "Guess I'm the last one ready."

"Not to worry. I finished up about five minutes ago," Shelby assured her. "So are we ready to head to town for breakfast?"

They all agreed and strolled out to Trent's truck then climbed in for the short drive to town. The mustang's backseat didn't provide enough leg room in the back for either of the men.

"I don't think we should discuss any of our suspicions or plans while at the restaurant. I'd hate to be overheard and misunderstood," Trent advised.

They all nodded in agreement.

"Well, I'll be. Y'all did come back. And you brought your brother and the future Mrs. Trent Meyers, too." Marcie grinned at them as they walked in the door of the restaurant. "Take a seat over there and I'll be right with you." She gave a hug to all of them as she handed Trent four menus to pass out among them.

The four obediently sat at their assigned location. Moments later Marcie arrived with four glasses of water and a pot of coffee. "All of you want coffee?" She turned up the first cup in front of Jason.

All of them said, "Yes," at the same time.

She grinned and filled their mugs before setting down the pot. "Do you boys want your usual?" Her pen poised over her notepad.

After placing their orders Lucinda asked, "Tell me about the wedding, Shelby. When is it?"

Shelby's eyes sparkled. "Three months. Plans are going fine. I'm an event planner so I figured it would be easy. Let me tell you, planning your own wedding is much harder than doing it for someone else. All the decisions. My goodness, it's overwhelming," her hand gestures almost toppled the salt and pepper shaker.

Lucinda laughed. "I can't imagine. Will it be a big wedding?"

"Of course. I've lived here all my life, Trent almost as long, and we know everyone. Cutting the guest list down to two hundred is a challenge. We're still working on that.

At least we have a few weeks before the invitations have to go out."

Trent grinned and patted Shelby's hand. "I'm here for support. Shelby makes all the decisions."

Shelby swatted his arm. "That's not true. You picked out the cake flavors."

"You're right, of course, sweetheart. I did manage to decide on spice cake with espresso flavored filling."

"Harrumph. All I have to say is this thing you guys are doing better not impact the wedding. I expect everything to be wrapped up well before so there is no stress and problems added to the ones associated with the wedding. Understood?" Shelby insisted as she gave Jason and Trent a stern look.

"Little brother, you have now been warned." Trent shook his finger at Jason with mock severity. "Finish up this effort and don't get in deeper trouble."

"Understood," Jason said with a grin and a salute to Shelby.

After they finished breakfast and said their goodbyes to Marcie and the other people at the restaurant, they piled into Trent's truck for the drive back.

When they arrived at the house, Trent put his hand on Jason's arm to stop him from entering while the women continued inside. "Hold up a minute, I have a question for you."

Trent seemed anxious. Like he had something serious to discuss. In spite of the joking at breakfast, Jason didn't make it easy. Why should he?

"The main reason I've been calling you is to ask you a question."

"Oh, what's that?" Jason asked the question deadpan.

"Would you be my best man at our wedding?"

Stunned at the request, Jason blinked a few times, but said nothing. Trent's expression changed from hopeful to disappointment then anger.

Trent said in a tight voice, "You can't tell me you already have plans. We didn't give you the exact date yet."

"Sorry." How come I had to say that, Jason wondered? "I mean, why do you want me to be your best man?"

"What do you mean, why? You're my brother. I like to think you're also my best friend. Who else would I ask?"

"Best friend? Since when?" He couldn't help the sarcastic repartee.

"Since always." Trent stomped closer to Jason until their noses almost touched. "What's with the attitude?"

"Attitude? I haven't heard from you more than four times a year the ten years you were in the army. Now you're back in the States and I'm supposed to drop everything else in my life and talk to you? Where were you when I needed someone to talk to? Tell me that? I know you were in the Middle East part of the time. I understand that part. You weren't there the whole time. Would it have killed you to pick up the phone?" Jason hated the pleading note he heard in his own voice.

Trent's stunned expression didn't make Jason feel better. He thought it would. Turning toward the front door, he heard Trent come up behind him. Jason turned back around to face him.

"Guess it's my turn to say sorry. I didn't think." Trent put both hands out and shrugged his shoulders. "I mean, I didn't realize you needed me back then."

"Didn't need you?" Jason stumbled over the word need. "Our mother had just died. I started college and my whole life changed."

"But you were here with all your friends." Trent's stunned expression surprised Jason.

"All my friends? How many do you think I had?" He couldn't keep the incredulity out of his voice. "Sure, there were people from the church. Mostly Mother's friends." He emphasized the word Mother. "Mine dropped me when I did nothing but go to school and take care of Mom. I'm the one who drove her to appointments, cooked, cleaned, worked in the yard. All the stuff she needed. When did I have a life? Never went to a school dance. Didn't have the money to take a girl out anywhere while in high school. Not to mention no time. Yeah, all my friends gathered around to talk and support me." Jason huffed while his face grew warm.

Trent had a stricken look on his face. "I didn't know. Hey, man, I really didn't. I thought you were at college having a great time. The times we did talk you seemed to be happy."

"That's what I wanted you to think." Jason shrugged. "Besides, things did become better after I started at USC and joined a fraternity." He glared at Trent. "They became my new family."

"So, can we start over? Start talking again? You're my only relative. I'd like us to be friends." The sincerity in Trent's voice came through loud and clear.

Jason glared at Trent for several moments. "I'll have to think about it. I do appreciate you helping us with this work problem." He felt his animosity toward his brother start to crumble. Although he promised Lucinda, he wasn't yet ready to totally forgive him.

"Sure, I understand. I still want you to be my best man," Trent said quietly. "Think about it then let me know. We have a few months before the wedding."

"Is it safe to come out now?" Shelby cautiously walked out the door, Lucinda following close behind.

"Of course." Trent gathered Shelby in his arms.

Lucinda stood there looking back and forth between the brothers. "Are we ready to continue our work or do you need some time?"

Her comment broke the tension. They all filed into the house and sat down at the table.

Jason felt more confused than ever. Trent seemed sincere about wanting a relationship with him. Maybe he should have spoken up back when his resentment started. But how could Trent have not understood what he was going through?

Lucinda started the conversation. "We told you how we managed to avoid being tailed here. Could you help us figure out a way to return to our apartments without being seen together?"

Trent asked with his eyebrows raised, "You don't think the fact you were both gone on Friday will alert them to the fact you are working together?"

Jason noticed her grimace at the possibility. "I hope not. We were careful."

Trent remained silent for a few seconds. Jason assumed he was considering the options.

"I think your best option is to drive from here to work on Monday morning. Jason can drop you off by your car." Trent looked toward his brother. "Jason, you need to switch vehicles with your buddy, right?"

Nodding, Jason said, "I told him we'd do it Monday morning."

"Perfect. Then you arrange to meet him someplace away from Lucinda and away from your work building. Chat with him for a few minutes after you trade car keys so it doesn't appear you and Lucinda arrived at the same time."

Jason begrudgingly acknowledged the wisdom in Trent's suggestion. "Fine. We can do that."

"What other questions did you come up with for me to ask my DEA contact?" Trent asked.

Lucinda asked, "How about connecting the federal agent with suspected terrorists? Is a snap shot of them together adequate?"

"I think I know the answer to that," Shelby spoke up. "A photo can be circumstantial or even Photoshopped. I do that sort of thing all the time on my web pages. It could even be a case of the agent being under cover or even a staged meeting in hopes of compromising said agent."

"You're right." Jason looked at Trent. "So what will suffice? Copies of emails? If they're in code, then how will we be able to corroborate anything?"

"That is going to make proving his complicity much harder. That's one of the questions I'll ask." Trent looked at Lucinda. "You said you found a file containing the email. Did you look to see if a list of code words and their meanings might have been in the same folder?"

Lucinda grinned and rolled her eyes. "Wouldn't that be perfect?" She paused and seemed to reconsider the comment. "I did not, but I'll look for it there and other places they may have stashed such information. After all, those kids didn't expect anyone to gain access to their computers. They thought they had a foolproof plan to wipe out the systems before law enforcement could crack it."

Trent looked at Lucinda. "Good. I'll make the call with these questions while you continue searching the files."

"What do you want me to do?" Jason asked Trent.

"At this point I think Lucinda needs to gather more info for us. Why don't you ask Mr. Harper to join us for dinner?" He grinned. "Then we can start the lasagna."

Shelby chuckled. "He's been talking about the lasagna since he woke up this morning. I'm heading over to my parent's house. Mom and I have some things to discuss about the wedding."

"We'll have dinner around six-thirty. Unless I call to tell you different, Shelby, could you stop on the way back and pick up Mr. Harper?" Jason asked.

"Of course, I'd be delighted."

"Mr. Harper was always a close friend to Mom then us, almost like family. Perhaps he thought it his Christian duty to help out. Now it's our turn to repay the kindness."

CHAPTER TWENTY-FIVE

Once again Lucinda set up her laptop on the kitchen table and went back to work on the files. She decided to look more closely at the folder containing the email messages saved by the college kids. Yesterday she'd only checked a few items before she had run out of time. The current plan included reading each and every file listed regardless of the name. The kids were smart enough to choose file names unrelated to the actual content.

While she searched, she heard Trent talking on his phone. Previously, she'd ignored his remarks. Now she listened while continuing her work.

"Helping out a friend. As a government employee he's in the middle of an investigation and has some concerns about one of the FBI agents."

A long pause passed before he continued. "He's shared the information with me he's gathered so far. Nothing that can be used in court, but I agree there appears to be a degree of concern. What information would his superiors need in order to open an investigation?"

Again, more silence as Trent listened to the response. "Right, I understand." He wrote notes on a piece of paper. "Thanks. Yes, let's keep this between us for now. I'll update you as I have more information."

Lucinda said nothing. Trent would apprise them all when they gathered again before dinner. She continued the mind-numbing repetition of her task for another hour before deciding to take a break. As she stood up to stretch and grab a drink, Trent spoke to her.

"Find something?" His voice startled her. "Sorry. Anything new?"

"Something to drink is all." She took a couple of steps away from the table and into the living room. "You've been quiet."

"Trying not to bother you," he acknowledged.

"Don't worry about me. I zone out when I concentrate on work. Something I learned a long time ago." Lucinda wandered into the kitchen as she carried on the conversation.

"Must be useful."

Taking a glass from the cupboard, she filled it with ice and water. "It is. Especially when you work in a bull pen type work space. Would you like something while I'm in here?"

"No, thanks. No need for headphones? That's what most people do now."

"Not required." As she spoke, the front door opened and Jason strolled into the house. "Ah, you're back. Will Mr. Harper be joining us this evening?"

"Yes. He is very excited. Insisted on bringing something."

They both sauntered into the living room and sat down.

Trent grinned. "That's like him. Let me guess, a salad."

"Since it will be fresh from his hot house, I couldn't refuse." Jason held up a bag. "I also scored fresh tomatoes. Exactly what I need to make sauce for the lasagna. Trent, did you get ahold of your contact at the DEA?"

"I did. He tells me we need to contact Washington's FBI Headquarters and talk to a Senior Inspector in the Office of Professional Responsibility, otherwise known as the OPR, when we have proof of a criminal act, or a violation of FBI policy. If we can provide emails between Shawn and the same people who contacted those college kids along with photos of their meet, it might be enough. It totally depends on the content of the emails. If there is some type of code, like between the students and those foreigners, then we need an explanation and how we figured it out. It could also be physical items such as documents, or even personal conversations. It's best if the exchanges are recorded. If we have conversations, then we need to be prepared to wear a recording device to tape future talks with Shawn."

"That's a lot of information we don't currently have," Jason pointed out. "What happens if we don't find it?"

"Let's worry about that after Lucinda finishes her search," Trent responded.

Lucinda let out a snort. "Thanks. No pressure."

Jason stood and spoke to his brother. "You wanted to learn how to make Mom's lasagna, right?"

"Absolutely." Trent jumped up. The two brothers tussled like teenagers as they moved into the kitchen area.

"Guess that's my cue to return to work." Lucinda set her glass of water next to her computer.

"Step one. Make the tomato sauce from scratch using fresh tomatoes. If you don't have tomatoes from a garden like these, then you can buy them at the store." He jabbed a finger in his brother's chest. "No canned sauce."

Trent huffed. "This must be why you said it would take a few hours."

Jason grinned without answering the question then handed Trent a knife. Placing a large pot of water on the stove he turned to Trent. "Let me show you how to peel and cut."

As the brothers set about making dinner, Jason decided to broach the subject of the trailer at Lucinda's encouragement from the previous day.

"I couldn't help notice you and Shelby have made a few improvements on the trailer. Do you plan to live here at some point?"

"Not anytime soon. However, Shelby wanted to make it habitable when we came for a weekend. Her words, not mine." Trent grinned. "Is there something you want to do with the place?"

"Honestly, I'd like to build a hunting cabin on the property in a few years. There are a few things here in the trailer I'd want to transfer, like some of the art in my room that Mom created." Jason had dreamed of doing that very thing for a couple of years now. He figured he'd have enough money saved in about four years to build a small cabin. As long as he did the work himself. "Since half of the land is yours, I didn't know if you'd want to build something else or keep the trailer."

"Honestly, I haven't given it much thought," Trent admitted.

After the tomatoes had been peeled, Jason showed Trent how to start the sauce.

Trent continued his comments. "The trailer is pretty run down. It's good for a weekend when we visit, but I wouldn't want to make it permanent. A cabin does sound more enjoyable."

"So you'd be willing to divide the land so we could each do what we want with our share?" Jason inquired.

Jason felt his brother's surprise at the request. "Do we need it to be that formal? I mean, sure, you can build a cabin. Like you said, the trailer is run down, but there are a few things inside I'd like to keep."

Jason supervised while Trent stirred the sauce.

For so long he expected Trent to give him a hard time about building a cabin, this reality made him step back and rethink his decision.

"I don't suppose it needs to be formal. As long as we agree," Jason admitted.

"We can look at the plot on paper and see what makes sense." Trent continued to stir the sauce as instructed. "As far as the trailer goes. I think removing it after we have something to replace it would be the most logical." Trent jabbed Jason with an elbow. "It will have to wait until after the wedding. The last thing I need to do right now is dig through a bunch of paperwork. Shelby'd kill me for doing anything other than make wedding plans."

Jason laughed at the comment. Happy that he'd spoken to Trent about his intention of building a cabin, he felt a weight lift from his shoulders. One down, one to go.

CHAPTER TWENTY-SIX

Lucinda stood and stretched while sniffing the air. "Wow, dinner is smelling fantastic. Is there anything available for a snack? Something light to tide me over until dinner?"

"Sure. There is some deli ham, pickles, cheese, as well as tomatoes I bought at the store before I knew Mr. Harper would be supplying some."

"Great." Her stomach rumbled. "Did you hear that? Now is the time for sustenance before it becomes louder."

Laughing at her, Jason said, "Help yourself."

"Hey, boss, anyway I can take a lunch break too?" Trent implored.

"Okay, okay." Jason threw up his hands as if in surrender. "We can stop for now. I think the sauce is ready. Turn the heat off and we'll pick up with step two after we eat."

The three chatted about inconsequential things as they pulled items from the refrigerator and cabinets to assemble their meal. It pleased Lucinda the two brothers seemed to be more relaxed in each other's company than when they reunited last night. She hoped the two would be completely reconciled before the weekend ended.

To avoid moving all of Lucinda's equipment and notes, they took their plates to the living room to eat.

After a few minutes of silence while they ate a few bites of food, Trent asked, "So anything new with the search?"

"I've discovered a few more emails, but nothing of significance. Your comment earlier about a description of code words has really taken root in my mind. I'm hopeful there is such a document. It could be helpful to prove some of our suspicions."

"I know it would. But we can't count on finding it so keep digging. If you think of anything else we can do to help, please tell us," Trent said before taking another bite.

"The one thing I know how to do is work on computers. If there is something else, I'm not sure I know it. Can you give me some suggestions?"

"What do you know about Shawn? Does he buy things someone with his income shouldn't be able to afford? What kind of car does he drive? Do you know where he lives? We can find the address, but what type of house or apartment is it?" Trent waved a pickle in the air. "Something above his means? If he is being paid by these terrorists for his work, then we might be able to prove it by following the money trail."

Lucinda considered his question. Slowly, she said, "He does wear really nice clothes. Though I have no idea how much they cost. Clothes aren't my thing. His car is nice, but nothing special like a Porsche or Ferrari." Lucinda finished her sandwich then stood to take her plate to the kitchen when Jason spoke up.

"Now that you mention it, I do recall some of the guys he hangs out with in my office talk about the number of vacations he takes. Not places like Myrtle Beach or Orlando, but fancy ones like cruises on the Mediterranean and skiing in Canada."

"Now we're getting somewhere. I'll see if I can track down some of that information." Trent deposited his dishes in the kitchen.

Jason said deadpan, "Are you trying to escape the cooking detail?"

Trent blanched. "What? No. No way, man. I really want to learn how to make that lasagna, but this weekend is all about helping you guys build a case."

Jason put up his hand as if to say stop. "Kidding, bro. I understand. Thought I'd yank your chain a little, that's all."

"I forgot how much you used to do that." Trent smiled. "I can have a friend do a search on Shawn's travel information without alerting him or anyone else. That will give us some dates and locations to check. If we're granted access to his bank information in the future, we'll have dates to review."

"Good idea," Lucinda said. "I suppose we'll need a warrant for that."

"Absolutely. If we don't do it all legally we can't expect the FBI to start an investigation."

They each proceeded to perform their tasks. In moments, Trent joined Jason in the kitchen.

"Okay, man. I'm ready to continue lasagna lessons." He rubbed his hands together.

"That was quick."

"Just a few emails to my buddy, now it's in his hands."

Jason and Trent worked alongside in silent companionship.

Sometime later Lucinda jumped up from the table. "I've got it, I've got it," she exclaimed.

"Shit," Trent said with gusto while placing his hand over his heart, "you almost gave me a heart attack."

At the same time Jason steadied the pan of lasagna Trent almost dropped as he prepared to slide it into the oven.

Lucinda gave them a chagrined look. "Sorry, guys. Those college kids were very savvy about working with criminals. They took a picture of a handwritten note containing a simple code. They stored it in this folder along with all the email correspondence. We were right about the few words we'd identified. This is perfect. We'll be able to do something now. Right, Trent?"

"Let me take a look." Trent sat down in Lucinda's chair so he could read the note. "This is good. Very good. They even took a picture of the envelope. Obviously hand delivered. They must have obtained some fingerprint powder. See that?" He pointed to some black smudges. "Those are fingerprints they dusted. You're right; these kids covered their tracks well. If Shawn finds out about this, I wonder what he'll do?"

"Can you have the fingerprints checked out?" Jason asked anxiously.

"Yes, but, I'll need to do this at the station." He looked at them both with a serious frown. "Not something I'm willing to send via my phone. This needs the personal touch to keep too many people from knowing about it."

Jason said, "Right. We don't want you getting into trouble because of this."

Trent waved his hand as if to dismiss the notion. "Don't worry about me. I'll keep all this on the down low."

"Great work, Lucinda."

"I'm relieved to have found something. Also, with all these emails I have more IP addresses to track. I recognize one as the coffee shop where those people who followed us contacted the students. I'm hoping at least one of these others is their home address."

"Then we could check to see if Shawn has any emails coming from the same addresses, right?" Jason asked.

"That's the idea. If we obtain a warrant," Trent warned.

"I'm going to track down these IP addresses," Lucinda said.

"Why don't you do that tomorrow? Mr. Harper and Shelby should be here soon. Let's clear off the table and set it for dinner."

She looked at her phone. "I didn't realize the time. Sure. I can continue the search later."

They all helped prepare for the evening meal. The atmosphere seemed celebratory. As they sat down for a drink, they heard a car approach the house.

"Must be Shelby and Mr. Harper. Good timing. I know Shelby will want a glass of wine."

Jason walked to the front door to open it and greet their visitor. "We're so happy you could join us this evening." He accepted the bowl of salad and a plastic bag containing various vegetables from the man's garden.

"Not half as happy as me, boy. I don't have many invites to dinner with such beautiful women. Who's this?" he asked motioning toward Lucinda.

Lucinda walked toward Mr. Harper with her hand out. "Lucinda Edwards. I've been hearing some interesting stories about you. You'll have to tell the other side."

Mr. Harper ignored the outstretched hand. "You must not be from the south, sweetie. We hug, not shake hands. At least old men like me do when there is a lovely young lady available."

Charmed by the old gentleman's flirting, she said, "I'm happy to oblige. Please take a seat and I'll grab you a drink. What'll you have?"

"A cold beer sure would taste good right now," the old man admitted.

"A beer it is then." Lucinda proceeded to the kitchen for his beverage.

Mr. Harper fell onto the couch as he looked Trent and Jason over. "Well, boys, it sure is good to see the two of you together. I hope you've settled whatever differences there have been between you."

Jason's face turn red. "We're working things out."

At the same time, Trent nodded.

"Good." Mr. Harper added a loud harrumph. While pinning Lucinda with his eyes he said, "So tell me about yourself, young lady."

She smiled at the old gentleman. "Jason and I work in the same building."

"At Ft. Jackson, right? Are you one of those budget people too?"

"Correct about Ft. Jackson. But I work with computers not budgets."

"Computers. Well, I don't have much use for them, but I suppose a lot of folks do."

"You're right about that, Mr. Harper. A lot of people do," Lucinda agreed.

They all chatted a while longer until Mr. Harper said, "How about some of that lasagna you promised? The smell is driving me crazy. Did you use your Momma's recipe?"

"Of course. It's ready to eat. Let's have a seat." Jason helped the old man off the couch and to the table.

Jason dished up the lasagna from pan to plates in the kitchen, the others ferried them into the dining area.

"I'll say the blessing if you don't mind," Mr. Harper said before the other dishes were passed around.

Jason and Trent nodded their approval.

"Thank you, Lord, for another day and the opportunity to break bread with these wonderful young men and their women. Help them to sort out their differences. We are all grateful for the food you provided and the hands that made it. Amen."

None of them said anything after they echoed Amen. Jason blinked a few times as he looked at Trent. Trent gave him a wry grin and shrugged.

Shelby, the ever-polite southern girl, broke the silence with talk about the upcoming nuptials.

At the end of the meal Shelby and Lucinda took over cleanup detail since they hadn't participated in making anything. Mr. Harper and the brothers moved to the living room to be more comfortable.

"I have to say your Momma would be proud of the way you cook, Jason." Mr. Harper said as he patted his stomach.

"Thank you. That's high praise. I remember you sharing meals with us the last couple of years I lived here."

"She always told me my tomatoes were what made the best sauce."

"I'd have to agree with her." Jason glanced at Trent with a smirk.

"It's getting late. Can one of you boys take me back? Missy should be calling soon," Mr. Harper requested.

"Your granddaughter?" Trent asked.

"Yes, she's a good girl. She calls most Saturday nights."

Trent stood up and offered the old man his hand. "Of course, I'll drive you over."

When Trent returned from his mission the dishes were done and they all sat in the living room to discuss their plan of action.

"Shelby and I will head back to Charleston after breakfast tomorrow. I'll drive over to the station and see if I can come up with a match on those fingerprints."

"Good. I'll continue to work on finding the physical addresses that correspond to the new IPs I found."

"Things are coming together. We've made a lot of progress this weekend. I look forward to hearing what you find, Lucinda, from your search on the actual machines those two college students used," Trent said.

"I wish I could figure out the purpose of the partially deleted code," Lucinda said with her eyebrows pinched together. "What were they trying to do with it? I feel confident it holds the key to their real objective."

"Right. Finding out who they are is the first step. It might provide us a clue to their motives, but not their end game."

"That's it for tonight. I'll fix breakfast in the morning," Jason volunteered. "What time do you want to leave?" He stood and turned to his brother.

"I'd like to be on the road by nine," Trent responded. "That way I'll be able to drop Shelby off at home then head over to the station. If all goes well, I should have some information by noon."

CHAPTER TWENTY-SEVEN

The next morning as Jason lay in bed he heard the women moving about and his brother starting the coffee. Better start cooking breakfast, he decided.

He slipped on a pair of jeans then headed to the kitchen. He put some bacon in a skillet and preheated the oven for the biscuits. He'd take a shortcut today and make canned biscuits, but he'd make his own sausage gravy. He pulled out another skillet for the sausage. Between checking the meat, he sipped the scalding coffee. Scrambled eggs would be easiest with four people so he cracked a dozen into a bowl so they'd be ready when he needed them.

"How can I help?" Trent sauntered into the kitchen, hair still damp from a shower.

"You can put the biscuits on the cookie sheet. I'll pop them in the oven when you're done."

"Sure thing." Trent did as instructed then poured himself and Jason more coffee.

Several minutes later Lucinda entered the kitchen. "What's for breakfast?"

Jason looked at her. "Bacon, scrambled eggs, biscuits, and sausage gravy. If you would set the table, everything will be ready in a few minutes."

Lucinda did as requested after she poured herself a cup of coffee then topped off Jason's mug. Shelby joined them and took the food as Jason dished it up then placed it on the table. They all sat down and started eating.

"When we finish I'll fill up a cooler for y'all to take with you. Don't worry, I'll put your share of the lasagna in there," Jason said with a chuckle.

"Perfect." Shelby agreed. "Lucinda and I can clean up the dishes. Trent, you start loading the truck."

"Yes, Ma'am," Trent said while giving her a salute.

They all laughed then finished their breakfast.

Once they completed their assigned tasks, they gathered around Trent's truck. Jason stuck out his hand for Trent.

Trent looked at the hand then ignored it in order to give Jason a bear hug. "Let me know when you decide."

Knowing the reference was to the request for becoming Trent's best man, Jason said, "I'll give you a call." Then Jason gave Shelby a hug as well.

Trent walked around to the driver's side. "I'll phone you as soon as I have information. Sometime this afternoon, I hope."

"We'll be waiting," Lucinda assured him.

After they left, Jason turned to Lucinda. "I'll head to the shower while you start your research again. But I don't want you spending all day working. You deserve a break. How about I show you around my hometown then stop some place for lunch?"

"That sounds great. We'll need to leave by four o'clock tomorrow morning in order to arrive for work on time. That means an early night for us."

"Indeed," he said as they strolled back inside the house.

Jason sauntered down the hall to the shower while Lucinda set up her computer on the recently cleared table. As he stripped down he thought about Lucinda joining him. Enough of that, he scolded himself. With significant effort he turned his mind toward thinking of ways to entertain Lucinda in Georgetown today. She'd worked hard all weekend and deserved a few hours of respite.

Trying not to interfere with her work, he stayed out of the dining and living room area. He transferred the laundry Shelby had tossed in the washer before leaving to the dryer. Putting the few clothes he'd worn during their stay into the washer didn't take long. He quietly entered the kitchen hoping Lucinda was "in the zone" as she called it.

The kitchen offered more options. He sorted through the pantry, arranging it to his liking. Then he wrote a list of nonperishable items to buy for the next time he came to Georgetown. Since when had he decided to come back? Perhaps Lucinda's insistence of the importance of family had penetrated his thick skull. To be truthful, he did want a relationship with his brother. At that moment, he decided to accept Trent's offer to be his best man.

With nothing left to do, he walked over to the table where Lucinda had started packing up. "Good. I was ready to suggest you stop for the day."

Lucinda looked up and smiled at him. "I'm ready to do something other than stare at a computer screen."

He shook his head. "I don't know how you do it for hours on end." He'd have never been able to do what she did. Wonderful didn't begin to describe her.

"It does make your eyes cross after a while," she admitted. "So what did you have in mind for this afternoon?"

"You mentioned you've been here before. What else did you see beside the Rice Museum?"

"We walked along Front Street where all the cute stores are located. We visited during the annual

Georgetown Art Festival." She sauntered into the living room and sat on the couch.

He sat next to her and put his hand on the one she held on her lap. "That's in May. The weather is usually good. Did you enjoy it?" He looked into her blue eyes.

"Absolutely. I noticed a poster about a boat tour going to Shell Island to collect sea shells. It sounded fun, but I've never been back to do that."

If he had a boat, he'd love to show her the coast line. "It is a great way to spend an afternoon. Sorry, they don't have tours on Sunday. Guess you'll have to come back another time to do that one."

"It's a date." Her face took on a reddish hue. "I didn't mean to…"

He smiled at her words. Words he wanted to copy. "I won't hold you to it. That is unless you …"

Lucinda smiled. "Yes, I believe I would."

Jason looked her in the eye. Was it his desire mirrored there or her own? He gathered her gently in his arms. When she wrapped her arms around him, he slowly brought his lips to meet hers, watching her reaction. The kiss started sweet then deepened to become more searching. Her mouth opened to accept his. The taste of coffee and bacon mingled with the minty flavor of his mouthwash. He'd never thought the combination as erotic, but with her it was. Before he allowed things to escalate, he pulled away with reluctance.

Lucinda seemed to be in a daze. He'd never seen her like that and smiled to think he'd caused it. "Maybe we should leave now before anything else happens."

"Right. Yes. That's a good idea," she said slowly, looking at his mouth in a way that made him regret his decision.

His phone rang. Taking a deep breath he pulled it out of his pocket and looked at the screen. "It's Trent. Maybe he has something for us." He clicked *accept* and put the speakerphone on so Lucinda could hear. "Did you find something already?"

"The fingerprints match another South Korean. A man named Yong Ro. At least his passport says he's South Korean. We definitely need to have the FBI find out if these people are suspected of being North Koreans or Chinese and whether they are on a watch list of some kind."

"Yes, we do. That means it is more important than ever we discover whether Shawn is on our side or not."

"Agreed. Let me know how things go tomorrow."

Lucinda spoke up before either disconnected. "Trent, I wanted you to know I found a couple of physical addresses associated with those IPs I've been checking out. Can you discover who lives there?"

"Sure. Those are public records as far as the owners of the addresses. If they are used as rental properties it will take a little more work. Not to worry, I can handle it."

Lucinda picked up a piece of paper from the table and read off the addresses.

"Okay. We each know what we need to do." Jason disconnected the call.

"Things are moving along in the right direction," Lucinda said.

"In more ways than one, I hope." Jason looked at Lucinda for confirmation.

She paused a few seconds before replying. "I believe they are."

Jason cleared his throat. "So let's head to downtown. There's a nice restaurant on Harborwalk I think you would enjoy."

"If they have fresh seafood, I'm in." Jason noted her enthusiasm with approval.

"Of course they do. The shrimp boats and other boats dock less than a block away. Can't get much fresher than that."

"Sounds great. I'll grab my purse then we can go."

As they drove to the boardwalk Jason considered the kiss they'd shared. He longed to do more than kiss her. Be patient. She needed to make the next move to be positive he wasn't crowding her.

"I have to say I'm really glad to be out in this beautiful weather. Thanks for making it happen," Lucinda said with fervor.

Jason chuckled. "Only the best for you. I thought I'd park a couple of blocks from the restaurant and enjoy the walk to it. There are a couple of shops you might enjoy looking through before lunch."

"Great idea. Thanks. I remember one containing some unique pottery by a local artist."

Jason grinned. "I know which one you're talking about. We'll stop there first."

As they browsed the merchandise in the shop, Jason told her about the turtles while Lucinda admired the pottery. "The turtles that nest in this area are called loggerheads because of their large heads. They are a very common variety of sea turtle you find up and down the Atlantic coast. They normally make their nests here in the Carolinas."

"Interesting." Lucinda picked out a chip and dip bowl. "I can use this when I have company. My friend Marcella will love it."

As they left the shop, Jason suggested, "Let's put that in the trunk so you won't have to carry it."

"Good thinking."

After they dropped off Lucinda's purchase, they strolled down the street stopping at the windows of the various shops and occasionally went inside if Lucinda wanted to inspect items more closely. Lucinda reached for his hand. He turned and smiled at her, accepting the gesture with delight.

"Where did you want to have lunch?" she asked.

"I thought we'd eat at The Big Tuna. It's casual and fun. Lots of locals. The restaurant has been around since before I was born."

As they entered the quirky restaurant, Jason's appearance elicited a similar response as when he walked into the Thomas Café.

"Hey, man, haven't seen you in ages. What's happening?" Bucky, the owner, asked as he slapped Jason on the back.

"Good to see you, too. Drove down from Columbia for the weekend and wanted to have some fresh seafood. I knew we'd find some here."

"You know it, brother. You're in luck. A table opened up outside."

Before they could take another step, a somewhat mechanical voice said, "Hello." Lucinda started at the noise.

Jason laughed. "Hello, Sassy." He pointed to the parrot who bobbed and weaved in her extra-large cage. Lucinda chuckled at the sight.

They strolled to the back door that opened onto the Harborwalk where a number of tables with umbrellas crowded the space. The breeze brought in a more pronounced scent of the salty air they'd been enjoying during their walk.

"So what do you recommend?" Lucinda perused the menu.

"Depends on how hungry you are. The she-crab soup is outstanding. And you won't eat a better shrimp po' boy. You need to be super hungry if you plan to tackle the flounder. It's massive."

"I see they have shrimp and grits. My favorite."

"You ate that Friday. Why not try something different?"

She chuckled. "Then a shrimp po' boy it is."

The waitress arrived. Jason spoke up. "I'll have the crab cakes and she'll have the shrimp po' boy."

"Sure thing, sugar. And what to drink?"

"Sweet tea for me." Jason looked at Lucinda. "Unsweet tea?"

At Lucinda's nod, the waitress wrote down her drink order. "Any lemon?"

"No thanks," they both chimed. The waitress smiled and hurried away.

"This is a beautiful view. Right on the water. The fantastic weather makes me not want to leave."

Jason chuckled. "This is the Sampit River. It flows into the ocean a short distance from here."

"Seeing all the boats docked is special. I'm also pleased the wind is blowing from the right direction and we don't have the smell from the paper mill today."

"Amen to that. Some of the boats are local and others stop here as they travel up and down the coast."

Lucinda's eyes lit up with delight. "Wouldn't that be fun? Travel by boat, stopping where you please."

"As long as you have nice weather it would be great," Jason agreed.

"Hey, don't ruin the picture," Lucinda said with a pout. "To think about boating in bad weather is off-putting to say the least."

"Sorry. When you live here year round reality does come in to play."

Their food arrived and they tackled their fare. Lucinda cut her po' boy in half so she could manage picking it up. Shrimp fell out and she stuffed it back inside. After her first bite she moaned with pleasure. "Good Lord. This is fantastic. You were right. Great suggestion." She took another bite.

"Glad you like it. Don't suppose you want to trade a bit of your sandwich for a bite of my crab cake."

"I thought you'd never ask. I've been wanting to try that, too."

Jason took her spoon and cut a large portion of the crab cake then dipped it in the remoulade sauce. He held it out for Lucinda. She opened her mouth so he could insert the delectable tidbit. Sliding the morsel into her mouth seemed more intimate than having sex. Her lips surrounded the offering and tugged on the spoon to capture each crumb. Once in her mouth her tongue darted out to capture the bit of sauce clinging to her lips.

Jason sat still as Lucinda closed her eyes in obvious enjoyment followed by a moan of pleasure. His mouth felt desert-like, his pulse quickened, and a heaviness in his groin made him grateful he was sitting down so she couldn't see his reaction.

"Jason, how fantastic. Here let me cut some of my sandwich for you." She proceeded to do exactly that and slid the section onto his plate. "I bet that sauce would taste great with my shrimp. Do you think they would bring me a small portion?"

The entire time she spoke, he watched her lips. Wanting to devour them like she'd done to her spoon. When he noticed her frown, he realized he owed her a response. What had she asked? Oh, yeah. "Sure, I'll grab the waitress's attention." He waved to the server who came over immediately to help them.

"Thanks. The problem now is I'll have an even more difficult time deciding what to order in the future."

Her grin made him want her even more. Returning to a normal conversation while his thoughts wandered to more erotic ideas with Lucinda took a major effort. "Yes, I have that dilemma each time I come back here."

Once they finished their meals and paid, they strolled along the Harborwalk that served as a dock and walkway adjacent to the Sampit River for the majority of the businesses along Front Street. Much to Jason's surprise, Lucinda linked her arm with his.

"You were lucky to grow up in such a quaint small town bucolic area. So serene and calm. I know it wasn't easy for you in high school with your mom's illness, but you seem to have a lot of friends. That had to be a big help."

"I suppose you're right," he admitted. "Not that it seemed that way at the time."

"Trust me. It could have been worse."

"That sounds like a voice of experience. Want to talk about it?"

Lucinda remained silent so long he didn't think she did.

With a deep sigh, she finally said, "Since you shared so much with me, I suppose it is only right I fill you in on my past."

CHAPTER TWENTY-EIGHT

"**I**'m not pushing. Tell me what is comfortable," Jason insisted. He found a vacant park bench adjacent to the Harborwalk and urged her to sit.

After a strangled laugh, she continued. "Nothing about it is comfortable. So, the first thing I remember is when I was about three or four. Only my Mom and me in an apartment. We'd just moved in. Mom cried almost every night. We shared a bedroom and a bed."

"So your Dad wasn't in the picture?"

"I have no memory of him. I have no idea who he is." What if he'd been looking for her all these years, she wondered.

"Oh, wow. That must have been tough."

"Mom must have been going to school and working. Trying to support us. An elderly neighbor took care of me part of the time. Sometime later I remember a big celebration. Balloons, cake, a sign I couldn't read strewn across our living room. Years later when I found the neighbor she explained it must have been when Mom received her Licensed Practical Nursing degree and a new job at a hospital. Mom seemed so much happier after that. I started school and had lots of friends to play with.

"After school each day our neighbor came to walk me back to our apartment building. She'd give me cookies and milk and let me watch TV at her place until Mom came home. The best times were when Mom didn't have to work and we'd go to the park. Then one day the neighbor came to school with a police officer and another lady. I've explained that part before. It's when they told me Mom had gone to heaven. Then I went to live with strangers."

"What happened to your mother?"

Lucinda stared off into space as she remembered that horrible day. "She'd been hit by a car in the hospital parking lot. Someone racing to the emergency room drove too fast and crushed her between their car and a parked truck. Something I learned later when old enough to understand."

Jason took her hand closest to him giving her some much needed warmth. "That had to be scary. What age were you?"

"Six. It was scary. Apparently they tried to find my relatives, but we didn't have any. At least not ones they could locate." She blew out a deep breathe. Relieving the events had been hard.

"You told me earlier how much your first foster family meant to you."

"I went from home to home for a few weeks until the Andersons took me." Her smile told him even now she liked the couple. "I count them as my first. They were wonderful. Very caring. They had a room especially for me. All painted pink with a white bed covered with stuffed animals."

"You said they became pregnant and after you acted up they didn't have a choice but to let you go. What did you mean by that?"

Lucinda crossed her arms, pursed her lips and looked down.

"I'm sorry, I shouldn't have asked." He reached over to squeeze her arm.

After a couple of minutes and a deep sigh, she continued. "They'd spoiled me and I let them know I didn't want a baby in the house. At first they laughed and assured me I would love my new sibling. Then I became angry and started being mean to them. I had tantrums, hit them, and refused to do what they told me. They took me to a therapist who tried and tried to assure me the Andersons would still love me after the baby arrived. I would not agree with anything the therapist said. After the baby was born, a boy, I tried to smother him with a pillow."

"Oh, no." Jason hugged her then kept her in his arms to comfort her.

"Oh, yes." Ashamed of what she'd done she took a moment to continue. "I didn't want to share my mom and dad with anyone else. Of course, they didn't have a choice at that point. They sent me to another foster care family. By that time, I had a reputation of being difficult. And I was. Nothing made me happy. I lashed out at everyone. I'd spend about a school year at each new foster home before they'd send me to another one. The next one a little worse than the one before. I finally figured that out when I was fifteen. So I stopped being such a pain. I started studying more at school. Stayed after school as long as I could so as not to go home. That's when I found computers. I joined the computer club and we could use the school equipment until five o'clock most afternoons. That way I didn't make it home until time to help with dinner."

"Is that when you learned how to hack?"

"Yep. Another foster kid doing the same thing as me. He'd figured out how to exit the controlled environment of the computers set up by the school. We'd spend hours trolling around and tagging graffiti on various websites."

"Graffiti on websites?" Jason gave her a puzzled look.

She chuckled at his lack of knowledge on the subject. "Exactly. It's when a hacker breaks into a website and leaves their mark to indicate they'd been there and could have done more than 'spray paint' their moniker. The more sophisticated the firewalls and security, the more challenging it became. We did it for the thrill."

"So that's what you meant when you talked about your misspent youth?"

"Yup. I honed my skill over a few years. Finding new friends who knew more than me and learning. Eventually I became the teacher. Sometime later the FBI caught us. The best thing that happened to me."

Jason quirked a brow as he stared at her.

"I broke into a government system." She shook her head at her stupid actions. "Those are the ones hackers love to penetrate. It's the ultimate badge of honor. Lots of street cred." She grimaced at the memory. "They didn't catch me during the actual hack, but afterward when I bragged about it in a chat room for hackers."

"Ah, showing off too much?"

"Yes, indeed. Then humbled when the FBI showed up at school and took me and a couple of others to their headquarters. You can imagine how my foster parents reacted."

"Off to another home?"

"Actually, no. The FBI gave us a choice. Go to jail or enter the army."

"What?"

"I know. I couldn't believe it either. Almost eighteen and about to graduate high school. I would have been on my own anyway since I would age out of the foster system. They wanted us to enlist in the army after graduation and work on computers. To keep other hackers out of the government systems then work with the FBI and other government agents teaching them the same skill."

"Ah, the old 'takes one to know one' adage. You said before there was more to the tale. So this is it."

"Exactly. I have no idea what I would have done if I hadn't been caught."

"You mentioned the neighbor who'd taken care of you when you were six. Is that when you went back to find her?"

"How did you know?" She looked at Jason with surprise.

"You said she told you years later about the party for your mom."

Understanding hit her. "Right. I did. Yes, about a year after I joined the army I went back to our old apartment. I knew the address because my mother had taught me our address and phone number in case of an emergency. The neighbor still lived in the apartment complex. In her eighties. Poor thing. Once she realized who I was, she invited me in for cookies and milk. The same as all those years ago." She felt a tear trickle down her face.

"So you don't have any relatives?" He brushed the tear away and put his arm back around her.

She appreciated his comforting embrace. "Not that I know about." She decided to share something with him. "I've wondered if my mother changed her name."

Jason's brows knitted together. "Why do you think that?"

"I did some digging a few years ago," she admitted. "There is no real record of her until I turned three."

"Have you done a DNA test?"

"No, although I've thought about it."

"Why haven't you?"

She shrugged and looked him in the eye. "Scared, I suppose."

"Scared about what?"

She threw up her hands. "What I might find. Maybe my dad abused her. Or maybe married to someone else and didn't want us. I don't know."

"I'll repeat what you told me." He gave her a squeeze. "Ask him the reason for all he did. His answers might surprise you. In your case, you need to find out who he is first."

She snorted at his words. "I hate it when someone throws my words back at me."

He grinned. "Yeah, I know what you mean. It sucks."

CHAPTER TWENTY-NINE

They sauntered toward the car. Lucinda's spirits were a bit low after sharing her memories. Surprised, Jason didn't immediately walk away after she'd exposed her secrets. She kept looking at him to gauge his reaction. Was he really okay with everything?

Jason stopped once they reached Front Street. "How about a walking tour of Georgetown?"

"Sure," she eagerly agreed, relieved at his apparent acceptance of her in spite of her flaws. "Being out in this fabulous weather beats sitting inside any day." Knowing he'd come up with the idea to boost her spirits made her smile.

They strolled down the historic streets shaded by old trees heavy with Spanish moss. Jason shared stories about several of the Revolutionary and Civil War era homes lining the streets. Lucinda slipped her hand in his along the way. As they ambled to Prince Street, he stopped so

Lucinda could read the plaque about the Champion Oak, over five hundred years old, which stood in the backyard between two homes.

"I've visited the Angel Oak in Charleston. This one is even older. How incredible," she said as they gazed at the magnificent specimen.

"Isn't it? When I was a kid, Mom knew some people who lived in the house adjacent to the tree. They let us climb it."

"Wow. That must have been fantastic."

"Fantastic doesn't start to describe the feeling. I don't think I really appreciated the honor until several years later."

She noted his bemused smile and suspected he was remembering childhood events. They continued their tour of the area.

"I can't believe how well the houses have been maintained. And the gardens. The scent of all the flowers is heady." She closed her eyes and took a deep breath. "The honeysuckle, roses, day lilies, and things I have no idea what they are. Magnificent."

"It wasn't always like this. The ups and downs of the economy affect everything," Jason explained.

"Of course it would. However, these houses were built with a quality new homes are not. So they can keep standing through some rough times."

"True. This is the last street for most of the homes. We'll return to the car via another route." He led her toward Front Street. "Would you like to stop and pick up something for dinner to take back to the house? Or have dinner at one of the restaurants in town?"

"I'm good with dinner at your place." Her voice became stern as she shook a finger at him, a grin sliding onto her lips. "But the lasagna is off limits. I want to take the leftovers home. What else is available?"

"I still have some veggies from Mr. Harper's garden, some lunch meat, and a few eggs."

"Then how about a chef salad with hard-boiled eggs?"

"Then we won't have any eggs left for breakfast," he pointed out.

"That's okay. We can pick up a breakfast sandwich at a fast food place after we hit the road. Considering how early we have to leave, I don't think I'll be ready for anything but coffee at that hour."

"Sounds like a plan," he agreed.

As they drove back to the house they chatted about inconsequential things. Like ordinary people on an ordinary date. Lucinda couldn't be happier.

Once they arrived at the house Jason put the eggs on to boil. Lucinda decided to wash her clothes since she hadn't expected to stay more than two nights. Once their small chores were complete they met back in the living room.

"How about a movie?" she suggested.

"Sure. What kind of movie do you want to watch?"

"I'm not too picky. The one type I don't like is horror shows. Anything else is fine."

"Then an action film it is," Jason said with a grin.

They both laughed as he selected something. He found one on a regular channel which meant commercials interrupted every few minutes. During those commercials, they tended to their minor chores. As they settled in for the last half of the movie, a steamy scene played that made Lucinda want to replicate it with Jason. What a cliché, she thought. She settled for snuggling with him. Much to her delight he put his arm around her and pulled her closer. At the end of the movie, they wandered into the kitchen. Lucinda chopped lettuce and cucumbers while Jason peeled the eggs, chopped and diced tomatoes, lunch meat, and a few other ingredients he pulled out of the refrigerator.

"I suppose we should go to bed after we clean up from dinner." Lucinda wanted to kick herself after the words left her mouth. She should have phrased it differently.

Jason blinked a moment as his face turned crimson. "Right. Four o'clock will come way too soon. Do you have an alarm clock or do you want me to knock on your door when it's time?"

Looking at him funny, she said, "I can set the alarm on my phone."

"Of course." He rolled his eyes. "I never think to use mine since I have a regular old-fashioned alarm in my room here and at home."

Clearing her throat, Lucinda nodded and began eating her salad. "Nothing is better than tomatoes from a garden. I wish I could have a small garden for vegetables."

Jason seemed to accept the change in topic when he said, "That's one thing I miss with living in an apartment. Mom always had a garden. I kept it up until I moved to Columbia."

They chatted during the meal and while clearing up the dishes.

"I'll say goodnight. Who gets the bathroom first tomorrow?" Lucinda asked.

"You take the hall bath. I'll use the master bath."

Lucinda wondered why things seemed so awkward. "Right. Goodnight."

Lucinda brushed her teeth and prepared for bed. All the while she thought of Jason down the hall doing the same thing. She wondered what he wore to bed. Anything? Those thoughts caused her temperature to rise. Trying to block out the image, she splashed some cold water on her face and thought about tomorrow's work.

CHAPTER THIRTY

Jason tossed and turned, unable to sleep, probably due to the early hour. He finally gave up and padded quietly into the living room, taking his phone with him. Sitting on the couch, he read the emails he'd accumulated over the weekend. Several minutes went by when he heard the refrigerator door open. When he looked up, his jaw dropped as he saw Lucinda's silhouette outlined by the fridge light. She didn't wear the T-shirt as that other time he'd seen her in sleepwear. This time she had on some silky looking nightgown that clung to her curvy body. It ended several inches above her knees. Should he speak so she would know of his presence? Stay silent and hope she didn't spot him? He didn't want to embarrass her.

She grabbed the milk then turned to snag a glass from the cupboard when she spotted him.

"Hey," he said softly.

"Hey, yourself. Guess you couldn't sleep either."

"Nope. Too early."

"Same here." She poured herself a glass of milk and returned the carton.

Much to Jason's delight she didn't seem embarrassed as she sauntered over to the couch and sat down next to him. He froze, not knowing how to respond. Well, at least his brain didn't know. The rest of him sure did.

Sipping her drink, she stared at him. He realized he wasn't wearing anything but a pair of gym shorts. She seemed mesmerized by his chest. He knew a lot of women didn't like hairy chests and he certainly had more than his share of chest hair. Lucinda, on the other hand, appeared enamored. At that realization, his body reacted even stronger. Her eyes traveled down and noticed.

A smile appeared on her face. She set her glass down on the coffee table. He watched as her nipples peaked. Scooting closer to him, she touched his arm, sending an electric current through his body. He leaned toward her and she met him halfway. He hesitated briefly before pressing his lips to hers. Lucinda kept her lips touching his as she moved to sit on his lap. He wrapped his arms around her and crushed her to his chest, inhaling her scent. Her moan of pleasure caused him to deepen the kiss and move his hands up and down her back. Her breasts pressing against his chest had to be one of the most erotic things he'd ever experienced. Although he longed for more, he'd be content with this if it was all she offered.

She put her hands on his neck. Not sure if she was trying to pull him away or keep him in place, he slackened his hold and their lip-lock. To his delight, she glided her tongue farther into his mouth then slid one hand down between them to play with his nipple. His immediate reaction caused Lucinda to break the lip-lock.

Breathing heavily, she continued the ministration to his nipple, drew back a couple of inches, looked him in the eye, and gave him a saucy grin. "I think you like that, don't you?"

"You know I do. What do you want next? Stop, play a while longer, or move to the bedroom?" He needed for her to know he gave her control of the situation. He respected her too much to take their next moves lightly. It wouldn't be a one-night stand for him. Her acceptance of him meant more than he'd previously realized.

"I'm enjoying myself a great deal right now." She paused a moment to run her tongue along her top lip, then grinned when he reacted. "But I want to feel your skin next to mine. No barriers. All of you. Would you like that, too?" Her question came out a bit breathless.

His response came without words. He picked her up and strode to the first bedroom, placing her gently on the bed. He hesitated to go further. "Are you sure? I don't want you to regret this tomorrow." He'd never forgive himself if she did.

"I'm sure. Before we continue, do you have some condoms?" Her eyes were large and shiny.

God, he hadn't even considered that. Shit. "No." After a brief pause allowing his brain to catch up, he shouted, "Wait."

He almost ran down the hallway to the master bedroom where he searched the nightstands. In the third drawer he opened, he found some. *Thank you, Trent.*

Returning like a warrior from a war, he held them up like a prize. "Yes, I do." He stopped in mid-stride when he looked at Lucinda. She'd shed the silky number she'd been wearing and sat in the middle of the bed completely naked. Glowing.

"Good. Now come join me." She patted the bed next to her.

He shucked his gym shorts and climbed onto the bed, setting the condoms on the nightstand within easy reach. He lightly touched her arm, moving his fingers up and down. "My God, you're even more beautiful than I thought." Before she could reply, he captured her mouth with his.

Each time he touched her she moaned with pleasure as she mirrored his movements eliciting the same response. Cupping her breast and thumbing her nipple, he smiled as she leaned into him. The lightness of her touch caused goose bumps to form on his arms although his body felt overheated. His shaft strained toward her. Not wanting to rush, he waited to see what else she would do. As much as he wanted to plunge deep inside her, he held back. The strain made beads of sweat break out on his forehead.

He turned on his side, lying face to face with her. He explored her body, learning her curves and mounds. She roamed her hands over his arms and chest, down to his waist and hip. Lucinda nipped at his lips then licked them, all the while looking into his eyes. "You know I don't date coworkers."

"I didn't know we were on a date." His caresses were growing bolder along with his heartbeat. He glided his hand over one nipple for a few seconds, traveled down her side to cup her ass and then draw their lower bodies close enough to touch. He wanted her to feel his desire.

Lucinda once again ran her tongue across her upper lip then let out a deep breath. "I suppose you're right. But I thought we might in the future." Her eyes wandered down as her hand reached between them to stroke his engorged penis. Looking up, that saucy grin appeared on her lips.

Releasing a groan of pleasure, he closed his eyes. "Yes, I want to date you. In the future. Will you make an exception? For me?" Jason took the hand he'd been using to caress her delightful derriere and slipped a finger into her honey pot from behind.

A startled gasp escaped her lips. Her languid eyes told him she enjoyed the surprise. "Ooh, yes, I think I will make an exception for you." She slung one leg over his, opening herself more fully to his access. "Kiss me."

Anxious to please her, he plunged his tongue into her mouth where she sucked on it, mimicking what he wanted to do with his cock in her pussy. He'd had sex with other women, but nothing could compare to this. Her responses were so sexy, open, and delightful. She seemed to be enjoying the romp as much as he. Romp? Not the right word. This constituted more than a romp for him. He wanted to share more than a great night of sex with her. No longer able to think further into the future than the next hour, he rolled her onto her back and started to plunge inside her. Stopping in time, he reached for a condom and held it out to her.

"Can you do this?" He gritted his teeth, knowing it would take all his effort not to come in her hands.

Nodding, she ripped the package open and slid the smooth rubber onto his shaft and guided him to her waiting womb.

After he slid inside, she whispered, "Don't move. Give me a minute."

He felt her muscles clenching and unclenching. More beads of sweat gathered on his brow as he strained to do her bidding.

"Okay. You were a bit larger than I expected. I had to adjust."

Startled at her explanation, he asked, "Are you sure?"

"Of course. We're good. Actually better than good. Fantastic."

He continued making love to her, receiving more pleasure than he'd ever experienced. He prayed he'd provided her with the same. As he slipped over the edge, he felt her join him at the same moment. Panting, he collapsed onto his back next to her. The two of them tangled in the sheets. His chest heaved as he gasped for air. The nights he'd dreamt of the two of them doing this didn't equal the reality. For her to give herself to him in this way made him feel humbled.

He reached over to touch her hand. "Did I please you?"

"You know you did. Wow. I haven't had a night like this in … well, ever. Not like this."

He couldn't help his feeling of pride. "Good. I'm glad. It's special between us. At least for me it is. I haven't felt like this before with anyone. When the danger has passed, I plan to tell everyone about us. Go on dates where all our friends know we're together as a couple."

"Why, Mr. Meyers. What a lovely speech." She smiled then turned serious. "Yes, I want to be with you. I want the world to know we're together. I don't do this type of thing unless I'm ready to commit to a relationship."

Pleased beyond measure, he kissed her. "I hate to say it, but we really need to grab some sleep if we plan to do any work tomorrow."

"You mean today?" she asked with an impudent grin.

"Good lord, you mean it's already Monday?"

She glanced at his nightstand. "According to your big green, glowing clock it is."

He rolled on top of her and kissed her again. "Thank you."

She wiggled under him. "You're more than welcome. I enjoyed it as much as you."

"I don't think that is possible." Her movements made his shaft twitch and grow.

"Believe it. It is." She caressed his ass with one hand then brought his head down toward hers with the other. Kissing him, she thrust her hips upward.

"You keep moving like that and we might have to start all over," he admonished.

"Promises, promises." She opened her legs and thrust again.

He took her challenge and plunged into her again.

CHAPTER THIRTY-ONE

At four o'clock, the alarm and music started. They both groaned as they untangled themselves from each other and the sheets.

"See what you've done?" Lucinda grumbled.

Chuckling, Jason responded, "Me? You were the one who started this."

"Yeah. So I did." For a non-morning person, she felt very perky. "We better start moving. Will you make the coffee?"

"Yes, I will."

Lucinda strutted toward the bathroom, giving Jason a great view of her ass. She glanced back at him and saw his intense stare. She wiggled her rear end then laughed when his jaw dropped.

After she dressed and had one cup of coffee, she helped Jason store the leftovers in the cooler and then filled two travel mugs.

Jason paused in packing his backpack to draw her attention as she quickly packed her own. "If you don't need anything in your bag for a few days, I think I should transfer it along with mine to my truck then to my apartment later. I'd hate to have someone notice me delivering your backpack to your place. I'm sure they'll be watching more closely."

"Good point. No problem with the clothes, I have plenty of others. I'll put my makeup and a few small items I'll need in my purse and computer bag."

Jason took their backpacks to load in the car while Lucinda tossed the sheets from their beds in the washing machine. Jason had already made arrangements with Shelby's mother for her to stop by to dry them and remake the beds. It would be too embarrassing for anyone to find the beds in the state they'd been in earlier. Her face felt hot at the idea. Had she really been so bold and wanton last night?

She walked out to the car as Jason locked the trailer door. Before she shut her car door, he stooped down and kissed her. She reached up and put her hand on his neck.

He released her too soon. "We better stop now if we plan to make it to work on time."

Feeling dazed, she said, "Right. Work. We have a lot to do."

Jason took off down the road. He pulled off after a little while and stopped for food as planned.

"I think I'll take two bacon, egg, and cheese sandwiches as well as hash browns," she said before he arrived at the speaker.

"Um. Have an appetite this morning? I wonder why?" he teased her.

As Jason placed their order, she noticed he ordered five sandwiches. "So who has the appetite?"

Chuckling, she saw his smile looked as big as the one she felt on her face. Munching as they drove to Ft. Jackson, Lucinda thought about the night they'd had. She'd had sex a few times. Not really too often. Certainly nothing like last night. Now she understood why her friends in serious relationships went on and on about their boyfriends or husbands.

After they finished eating, Lucinda took their wrappers and stuffed them all back into the bag and put it behind her seat.

"We need to go over our plan for later today," Lucinda said. "I'll have my team start looking at the files as soon as we settle in. I've already divided them up to make sure my section has the one with the email containing the code word description as well as the set of IP addresses. When I discover it, I'll talk to Marge about providing the information to the FBI's Office of Professional Responsibility. Hopefully, she won't be suspicious as to how I did all that in such a short time period."

"How do you plan to explain how you know about the OPR?"

"I've been thinking about that. She knows I worked with the FBI on previous projects when in the army. If she asks, I'll explain OPR is the right office to send the information about Shawn and open an investigation."

"That makes sense to me."

"What about you? Do you have any specific projects to work on?"

"I'm sure after being gone on Friday there will be plenty of work waiting. The key will be to concentrate on anything knowing we have so much on the line."

"So what do we do about us?" Lucinda asked.

"Us? You mean being seen together?"

"I mean more than being seen together."

"Of course, but right now it is important to stay the way we were before last night. Until the danger part of this is over," Jason cautioned.

"When will that be?" Lucinda noted the despair she felt creep into her voice.

Jason reached over and took her hand in his. "Hopefully, not much longer than two or three days." He looked at her with desire. "I don't think I can keep up the pretense that I'm not crazy about you."

Appreciating the confirmation of their mutual feelings, she said, "Same here. I'd be proud to be seen with you as my date." She wanted to say significant other. Was it too soon?

"Even though we're coworkers?" Jason said with a teasing tone.

"Even though." She returned his smile. "Since we work in different departments, we're more like fellow employees of a large organization."

"Splitting hairs?" He chuckled.

"Hey, it helps my conscience." In fact, her conscience didn't bother her at all. Jason would be worth changing jobs if an office policy required it. Thankfully, it didn't.

"Then by all means think of it that way."

They continued their banter until Jason suddenly pulled off the road a few miles short of Ft. Jackson.

"Why are we stopping?" Lucinda frantically looked around them.

"So I can do this." He released his seat belt and put his hand behind her neck, pulling her toward him as he leaned closer. He proceeded to kiss her until she had no thoughts in her head. Releasing her, he drew back a few inches. "I'm not sure when I'll be able to do that again, so I wanted to make sure you remember I still want you."

Dazed for a few moments, Lucinda finally said, "Message received. I wouldn't have forgotten, but I certainly appreciate the reminder." She grinned and gave him a light kiss before he put his seat belt back on. Within a few minutes, they pulled into a gas station to fill up before returning the borrowed car. Lucinda gathered the trash from the car and stuffed it into the garbage can between the pumps.

Reaching into the back seat Lucinda plucked their hats and handed Jason his. "Just in case our shadows are watching as we drive through the gate. I'll pretend to look in my purse while we go through."

"I hate that we have to stop and show our IDs to the guards. It could give them a better chance to spot us together," he said with a worried look.

"It seems unlikely they'd be so close as to see us." After a moment's thought, she said, "Unless they've tapped into the cameras at the gate."

They looked at each other with concern.

"Holy cow, I hadn't thought about that before. They could easily have hacked into the system," Jason exclaimed.

"Since they've been following us, they probably didn't check the cameras until we both disappeared this weekend. Great. Now what should we do?"

"We can't do anything about it except wear the hats and sunglasses," he pointed out. "At least we're not in our own vehicles so it could take them a while to figure it out. By that time, maybe we'll have everything we need to have them arrested."

"Today's mission seems even more critical than before," Lucinda said.

They drove through the gate and to their work site without incident. Neither tried to discover whether their shadows watched for them. It seemed more important to concentrate on hiding as much of their faces as possible.

Jason dropped Lucinda off near the gym entrance to avoid attention. He then drove to his building to switch vehicles with his coworker.

Lucinda did the research on the IP addresses and matched them with the physical addresses. As she pulled up maps to determine their locations, she realized there were a few residential locations mixed with various coffee shops in the area. One address corresponded to the address on the driver's license of one of the Koreans. Another was Shawn's. Bingo. That was what they needed to convince the FBI to tap Shawn's phone. At least, she hoped it would.

Around eleven o'clock, Lucinda pretended to discover the email defining code words. She called her boss. "Marge, I have something important to share on the investigation."

Sounding frustrated and overwhelmed, Marge replied, "Can it wait until the end of the day when we update the FBI?"

"I'd rather not. It seems too important." She stressed the word important.

Marge sighed. "All right, then. I have a few minutes before my next meeting. Come on over."

Rushing to Marge's office, Lucinda knocked then opened the door. "Thanks for seeing me." Lucinda showed her a copy of the note she'd found.

Marge glanced at the document. "This is a great discovery. However, it could have waited until this afternoon. Why the rush?"

"I have something else even more important."

"Really?" Marge gave her a stern look. "What's up?"

"I've had a couple of discussions with Jason Meyers. You know, the guy from budget who started this whole investigation."

"Of course I know Jason. What were you two talking about?"

"Remember the strange comment Shawn made the other day when you and I were on the phone? On a hunch, I asked if Shawn spent time in the budget office."

"Why would you ask that question?" Marge gave her a puzzled look.

"Because someone had to infect all those computers with that virus in a way that required direct contact. I thought he might be a candidate."

Marge scowled at her. "That's a serious accusation, Lucinda."

"I know. That's why I didn't plan to bring you the information until I obtained more evidence."

"What kind of proof do you have?"

"The day we determined the machines were infected, Shawn visited the budget office. All budget personnel had mandatory training so he could have been alone. His reason for the visit was to have lunch with some of them. If he arrived early, he would have had plenty of opportunity to take a flash drive and download the virus."

"Why would he do that? He's an FBI agent. You'll need more than that for me to make the call."

"Those IP addresses between the college kids and other people. I suspect the *other people* are the ones who thought up this whole scheme. They are the real terrorists. I tracked the IP addresses to several coffee shops and a couple of residences. One of those residences is Shawn's."

Startled, it took a few moments for Marge to digest the information. "Good lord. You think he's involved? What are you suggesting?"

"I'd like you to call Washington's FBI Headquarters and talk to a Senior Inspector in the FBI's Office of Professional Responsibility, also known as OPR. It is my understanding the office is the FBI's equivalent to Internal Affairs. I'd like them to obtain a warrant to look at his bank account or tap his phone. I know this is a lot to ask."

"Yes, it is. I don't think there is enough proof to request a warrant for his bank account. We can call and ask. If Shawn has a government issued phone, then there is no expectation of privacy and they should be able to gather information. Assuming they agree with your theory."

"Even if they don't agree with it, we have to urge them to do it to prove Shawn's innocence. Otherwise, the whole Columbia FBI department could be suspect."

"When you put it that way, they might agree," Marge responded in a reluctant voice. "All right. I'll do it."

"Thank you, Marge." Relief flooded through Lucinda. Now they had to convince the FBI.

After their review, Marge dialed the number of the OPR. "Director, thank you for taking my call. Something important has come up I would like to discuss."

Marge quickly explained the circumstances and asked for their cooperation. She sent him the electronic evidence they'd gathered to date. After much debate, the director agreed to look into the matter. He also agreed to contact Shawn's boss in order to keep Shawn's knowledge of further developments to a minimum until his involvement was proven or disproven.

Lucinda was elated they'd accomplished the mission without Shawn being any wiser. At least for now.

"Thank you for everything, Marge. I hate to think Shawn is guilty, but if so, we need to find out. This is the only way I can see how to do it."

"If I didn't agree with you, I wouldn't have made that call. I agree Shawn's reaction on the phone the other day was suspicious. At the same time I would never have dreamed he had a part in all this. With your additional information, it now seems likely. Good work. Speaking of work, I have a lot to do and so do you. Let's get back to it."

Dismissed, Lucinda left the office with hope the whole thing would be wrapped up in a few days. Then she and Jason could have a real life together.

Back at her desk, she decided to delete all the stuff she'd copied to her personal laptop for her investigation. No need for it now. She'd do the rest of her work on the desktop at her cubicle and the infected computers. After that task was completed, she spent the afternoon working to uncover more from the compromised computers. Those pieces of code still bugged her. What were they all about?

A few minutes past her normal time to leave, she found what she'd been looking for. Deleted portions of code that matched up with the partial. *No. It's not possible. Why were they looking for that on our systems? We don't have anything to do with that at our installation. Do we? There could be some classified system I don't know about. For security it would be on different servers at a different location at Ft. Jackson. Even though I have a Top Secret Clearance, I wouldn't have a need to know so there could be something out there. It doesn't matter. The fact these people are looking makes me concerned about the possibility.*

Taking her newly found information she once again phoned Marge, hoping she too worked late.

"You've been busy today. What do you have now?" Marge asked.

"If you have a minute, I'd like to explain." This couldn't wait until tomorrow. Every minute could be important.

"You sound very serious. Come on over."

Walking toward Marge's office, she glanced down at the printout. How was it possible?

"Did you find something more damning to Shawn?" Marge inquired.

"No. Nothing more about him. It's actually scarier."

Marge blinked at her statement. "What?"

"The code I told you that had been partially deleted. I found the rest of it. The deleted part."

"And what does it do?" Marge asked slowly.

"It was a search. Of course, I already knew that part. But I didn't know what they were searching for. This whole time I think we all believed they wanted to siphon money from multiple weapon systems. At least, I know I did."

"True," Marge admitted. "But you found something else?"

"Yes. They're trying to discover how we created our electromagnetic pulse."

"An EMP?" Marge gave her a puzzled look. "We don't have one. Wait." She tilted her head and gave Lucinda a serious look. "Do we?"

"I don't know if we do or not," Lucinda admitted. "Actually, it doesn't matter. What matters is the fact they are looking for it. Are we the only facility they've breached? What if they did find it somewhere? If they steal it, then what?"

Marge threw up her hands, then stood and paced around the small office. "Who are these people?"

"I'm hoping the contacts Shawn has will tell us." Knowing she couldn't share her assumptions about the Koreans right now felt awful. Trent would know how to provide the information to the FBI.

Marge punched in some numbers on her phone. "I think I need to contact the FBI again. This time I'm going to call on a secure line. I don't want anyone else knowing even a hint of this. If the terrorists, or whoever these people really are, have hackers in other places doing this same thing, they might find the information somewhere."

Marge contacted the director in Columbia, telling him they would call at nineteen-hundred hours on his secure line. No additional information provided. Lucinda stayed with Marge as they went to the emergency operation center where the secure phones were located and maneuvered through the process to make the call.

"Well, ladies, you must have something really hot if you're calling on this line. Is this about your contact with OPR? If so, I assure you Shawn will not have further knowledge of this effort until his name is cleared." His voice indicated his displeasure. "Although I'm stunned his involvement is possible. I will wait for proof."

Marge spoke in a stern voice. "We believe we do have something hot. It has nothing to do with Shawn. At least, we don't think it does."

They provided him all the information they had about the search. He assured them he would contact the appropriate people to determine if such a system existed and pass on the critical intelligence. They would probably never receive confirmation of whether their input was critical or not. They'd done what they could and would leave the rest to others.

As they returned to their office area, Marge said, "You realize we can't discuss any of this with anyone, right, Lucinda?" She gave Lucinda a look reserved for serious offenses.

"Of course. I won't say a word." The importance of security had always been her top priority.

"Good. It could mean your clearance would be revoked if it came out that you did," Marge cautioned.

"Understood." Lucinda knew all too well what happened to people who shared Top Secret information. After all, she was the Information Assurance Manager. "Thank you for believing in me."

Marge waved her hand as if in dismissal. "That goes without saying. You're a great asset to our team."

Lucinda knew she wouldn't be able to tell Jason what she'd found. She could tell him she found something important and had made appropriate calls. He'd understand her dilemma; he had a Top Secret clearance too.

She pondered the idea of the existence of a weaponized EMP. A device that could disable any and all electronic devices within a specified range was indeed possible, but how realistic? Sci-Fi flicks abounded with the scenario. The dark web contained a host of information. Mostly conjecture, very little truth. She didn't believe Ft. Jackson, South Carolina, would be the place something like that would be researched and developed. Of course, that could be the exact reason Ft. Jackson was selected.

As she shut down and packed up her computer to leave, she suddenly felt exhausted. It had been a long day and she looked forward to reheating the leftover lasagna for dinner then crashing. Making her way to the break room where she'd put the treat in the refrigerator, she snapped it up and put it in her bag. She sent Jason a quick text telling him she'd finished up and was headed home. Telling him they'd talk tomorrow. As she drove off post, she spotted her shadow start his tail. *Sorry, guys. Too late. You can't do anything now.*

Pulling up to her apartment, she gathered her laptop, purse, and leftovers. She heard the ding of her phone indicating a text. Since it came from her throw-away phone, she knew it would be Jason. As soon as she unloaded her things inside her apartment she'd read it. With her hands full, she started up the stairs. As she put her foot on the second step, someone behind her shoved her. Hard. Dropping everything in her hands, she kicked back with her right leg while spinning to face her attacker. The man dodged her poorly aimed foot, grabbed her ankle with his left hand, and aimed a gun with his right. She noted the silencer attached to his weapon.

"Stop. I'll shoot you right now." His whispered voice was full of anger.

She realized he was one of her shadows when she recognized his face from the driver's license photo. Min Ro. She'd seen it over the weekend. His accent confirmed his Korean roots. Whether North or South she didn't know.

Above and behind her, a woman spoke in Korean then switched to English. "Stand up and put your hands behind your head. Don't say anything or I'll shoot you and anyone else who tries to help."

The woman must be Mee Pak, Lucinda realized. If she screamed, would someone help in time? Would she endanger others? Did Mee Pak also have a weapon? Probably. All these thoughts went through her head in a split second. She decided to not take a chance and do what they ordered.

Min Ro spoke to Mee Pak in their language. She moved down the stairs and then patted Lucinda's legs and waist to make sure she did not have a weapon. Fortunately for Lucinda, Mee Pak missed the burner phone in her back pocket.

Mee Pak picked up Lucinda's purse which contained her work phone and laptop then shoved a gun into her back. "Start walking. Put your hands by your side. Keep your mouth shut."

They proceeded to take her to the Camry. The man drove with Lucinda and the woman in the back seat.

"What do you want?" Lucinda asked.

"Shut up. You'll know soon enough," Mee Pak replied.

"Did you take the battery out of her cell phone?" Min Ro asked.

"Of course. As soon as I secured her."

When the woman pulled out a zip tie, Lucinda remembered to cross her wrists and clench her fists so she would later be able to slip out of them. As Mee Pak put a scarf around Lucinda's eyes, she started counting, trying to keep track of the time as well as direction. Her army training hadn't helped during the kidnapping, but perhaps it would keep her alive. If given a chance to communicate with someone, she'd be able to pass along information as to her location. Knowing the address of the people who kidnapped her helped her realize their travels took them toward that destination even though her eyes were covered. After several minutes, the car stopped.

She heard a garage door open then the car moved a few feet and stopped again. The garage door closed. No one would see a woman tied and blindfolded walk into the house. Min Ro grabbed her out of the car and marched her a few feet before she stumbled up two steps as he jerked her into a building. He shoved Lucinda into a chair then ripped the blindfold off.

Lucinda felt smug with the knowledge Mee Pak missed her burner phone in her back pocket. They hadn't expected a second one. Lucinda's blouse was long enough to cover the obvious bulge. The phone she used to communicate exclusively with Jason remained on her person. He'd find her. If they left her alone, she'd be able to call him after she slipped out of the zip tie.

Confident time would solve her problems, she asked, "What do you want from me?" She forced herself to appear scared, knowing the man at least would expect it from a frail American female.

"I told you to shut up." The man slapped her face.

"The blue-eyed devil told you not to harm her," Mee Pak snapped.

"I don't take my orders from him," the man replied.

The coppery taste of blood filled Lucinda's mouth. Instead of making a snarky comment about the lack of power behind the slap, she opted to continue her helpless female act.

"Don't hurt me. Please don't hit me again," she begged then whimpered. "What do you want? Who are you?" She managed to squeeze out a couple of tears.

Min Ro demanded, "You are trying to track the code left on the computers of those idiot children."

Since it wasn't a question, she nodded.

"What have you found? Who have you told?" the man screamed.

Flinching and blubbering for effect, she stuttered, "N-nothing. I tracked the IP addresses to a coffee shop. I'm still trying to figure out what the code means. I haven't told anyone. What good would it do?"

Min Ro looked to Mee Pak with a sneer. "I told you this worthless *woman* would not find anything. This is a waste of time. We should shoot her and be done."

"No. The blue-eyed devil will be here soon. He wants to make sure she knows nothing."

Mee Pak switched to Korean so Lucinda could not understand their conversation. The man seemed more agitated the more Mee Pak spoke. He shook a fist and pointed to the scarf. The woman then tied it across Lucinda's eyes, putting her once again in darkness. She wondered what that meant. Mee Pak then zip tied her feet to the chair, removed the zip tie from her hands only to put them behind her and slip on another zip tie. She heard the two arguing, but they moved into another room. She debated on whether to break her hands free. Lucinda decided against it since the couple each had a gun and she might not be able to escape before they turned on her. Min Ro didn't seem opposed to shooting her.

So who was this blue-eyed devil? Shawn? Is that why they put the blindfold on again? It wasn't long before she heard a door open then close. Both people stopped talking for a moment. A third person had arrived. The voices began whispering together in the other room. The new voice was male, definitely American. They'd started speaking in English again although she couldn't hear enough to make sense of their conversation.

The three walked into the room she occupied. Once again she spoke in a frightened voice. "Who are you? I've told them I don't know anything. Please let me go. I won't say a word."

"If I believed that, I would."

She couldn't decide if the muffled male voice belonged to Shawn or someone else. "Ask me any question you like," she insisted. "I'll tell you what I know."

"You say you tracked the IP addresses to a coffee shop, correct?"

"That's right. I did." She realized he must be covering his mouth with a cloth to keep her from recognizing his voice. Someone she knew. It had to be Shawn.

"Did you find any others?"

"Y-yes, I did. Other IP addresses. I haven't had time to track them down."

"So, what about the code? Did you find out what it did?"

She decided to tell them one thing that wasn't important, but perhaps it would satisfy them. "I know it is a search. I haven't figured out what the search is designed to find. Is that what you want to know?"

"Ah, so you do know something."

"That's it. That's all I know," she insisted in her scared voice. "A search for some unknown something. What good is that without finding out what it is?"

"You'll continue the search. Right?"

Shaking her head furiously, she said, "Not now. I promise. I won't look any further."

The man sighed. "I wish I could believe that. I don't. Not any more than I believe this act that you're scared and helpless."

"What are you planning to do to me?" She gave up the act. Her question came out as a demand, not a request.

"That sounds more like you," the man said with a sneer in his voice. "Guess you aren't as good as you thought if you haven't found more."

Someone who knew her. Definitely Shawn.

She knew he baited her. She decided to play along. "I'm plenty good. Given enough time I can figure it out. What are your plans for me?"

"I won't do anything. But I can't say the same for my colleagues. They have something special in store for you." His voice indicated she wouldn't be pleased.

He spoke to the Korean couple. "I agree she hasn't discovered anything more than we already know. She's so arrogant she would be bragging about it if she did. There is still a chance she will in the future. Now you've taken her, she'll make it her mission. You know what needs to happen. I told you not to leave any marks. Her value goes down when you do." He walked away then she heard a door open and close.

What the hell did that mean? Her value went down? Value to whom?

Mee Pak spoke Korean to her partner. He made no response, but Lucinda heard him walk away. She figured this would be her one chance.

In a loud voice to cover her movements, she moaned and wailed. "Nooo, please. Don't do it. I won't say anything."

At the same time she bent forward to position herself better to break the zip tie. With a swift and firm motion she snapped off the ties from her hands then reached out to grab the woman she believed was within reach. Only managing to snag the woman's clothes with her right hand, Lucinda tore the scarf from her eyes with her left hand.

Mee Pak pointed the gun at Lucinda, still bound at her feet. Lucinda lunged forward to knock the weapon out of Mee Pak's hand before she had a chance to use it. Then everything went black.

CHAPTER THIRTY-TWO

"I'm telling you something is wrong," Jason insisted.

Trent spoke calmly. "I believe you. Start from the beginning and tell me everything."

"Lucinda and I made it to work this morning. I received a text around eight tonight saying she was leaving work and we'd talk tomorrow. Then I sent her a text asking her to let me know when she arrived home safely. It's nine o'clock and she hasn't answered."

"Did you agree to contact each other at a specific time?"

"No." Jason ran one hand through his hair.

"Did she say she wanted to talk when she arrived home?"

"No, that's why I texted her. She should be home by now. I called on her work phone. No answer." He paced up and down his living room, unable to sit still.

"Did you call her on her regular cell phone, not the burner phone?"

"I didn't think it would be wise. Can you track the location of both phones?"

"I can if she's in imminent danger," Trent agreed. "Do you think that's the case?"

He stopped dead in his tracks. "Yes, I do," he said, his voice full of emotion. "This isn't like her. She would at least have responded to my text. You have to help me find her." He couldn't help the pleading tone of his voice.

"Okay, okay. I understand. She could be in trouble. Did the van follow you home as usual today?"

"No, I haven't seen it." Jason began his pacing again.

"Hmm," was Trent's only response.

"What do you mean by that?" Irritation filled him at Trent's lack of action.

"Nothing. Nothing," Trent assured him. "I'm trying to figure out if that is a good sign or not."

Jason lashed out verbally. "I'm telling you it is a bad sign. I'm trying to make sure Lucinda is all right. We have to find her." He continued pacing in his increasingly smaller living room.

Trent barked out an order. "First, go over to her apartment and see if she's there."

He stopped to consider Trent's comment. "What about the people who follow us? What if they are surveilling her?"

"You said you weren't followed. When you approach her complex, check to make sure the other vehicle is not in her parking lot. Then look for hers. If it's not there, then go to her door and knock. Maybe she fell asleep or something," Trent explained in excruciating detail.

Slapping his hand on his forehead, Jason muttered, "I can't believe this. You want me to waste time running around?"

"Calm down," Trent said again. "We'll find her. I can't trace a phone belonging to an adult with no good reason. There are laws about privacy. Do what I asked and in the meantime I'll start the ball rolling to figure a way to cut through the red tape."

Raking his hand through his hair, Jason replied, "Fine. Fine. I'll drive over there now."

Irritated at Trent's nonaction, Jason took the time to grab his 9 mm semi-automatic and a box of ammo then ran out of his apartment. He jumped into his car and burned rubber out of the parking lot. He slowed down as he entered Lucinda's apartment complex. Cruising by the visitor parking area, he didn't spot the Camry or the van. He made one more pass before driving closer to the area reserved for tenants. There. Lucinda's car. So she'd made it home. Why no return text? He pulled in a slot without caring it was designated for handicapped parking.

As he started to rush up the stairs, he noticed something messy on the third tread. He paused a moment to discern what it was. *Oh My God! Leftover lasagna.* Looking down, he spotted the container they'd put it in while in Georgetown. Now he knew for sure she was in trouble. Someone must have accosted her on the steps. He sprinted to her door and pounded on it, calling her name several times. Not receiving an answer, he pulled out his phone to call his brother as he hurried back to his car.

Before Trent could say anything, Jason spat out, "She's been kidnapped."

"What? How do you know?" Trent replied in a startled voice.

"Her car is parked in her usual spot at her apartment complex. She doesn't answer her door or her phone. And there is lasagna on the steps."

"Did you say lasagna?"

"Yes. She had some leftover from the weekend. She had to be taking it upstairs when attacked and dropped it on the stairs."

"Normally I'd say you were crazy, but I know how she loved that lasagna. Did you see the container?"

"Yes, below the stairs like it fell there. It's from our house."

"She would at least have picked that up if she'd dropped it accidentally." Jason heard the concern in Trent's voice. "All right. I'll finish the paperwork and let you know when we find her."

Jason froze, stunned for the second it took him to understand. "Wait a minute. What do you mean when you find her? Aren't you planning to tell me where she is?"

"I can't do that. You're a civilian." Trent's tone had changed to his cop voice calling the shots. "This is a police matter. You could be in danger."

"I might be in danger?" His voice grew in volume until he shouted the next words. "She's in danger. I know she is. You have to let me know where you find her phones. I can meet the cops there."

"That's not how it works," Trent insisted, keeping his voice low and calm.

Jason continued to shout into the phone. "It sure as hell better work that way. I can't lose her." Jason took a deep breath to try to keep his voice calm. He lowered the volume. "I have to be there for her. She needs me and is counting on me."

"Look, you're a civilian," Trent explained. "You could endanger her more if you go in there with no training, no plan, and no weapon."

"You can't do this to me. You owe me. I have a gun and I know how to use it. Remember all those hunting trips we took? I still hunt and practice at the range to keep up my marksmanship." He'd say anything to stay in the loop.

"I owe you? Why do you say that? Never mind. We're wasting time. All right," Trent gave in. "I'll call you when I have the information."

After disconnecting, Jason climbed out of his truck and paced around. How long would this take? Where should he go? He couldn't sit in the parking lot waiting. He climbed back inside the cab and drove away. With no destination in mind, he initially headed toward Ft. Jackson.

As his thoughts cleared, he realized one place he could try. The address Lucinda had discovered from the IP address. The one that wasn't a coffee shop. Maybe they took her there. He'd need to be careful. Trent had that right. Fortunately, he remembered the address and plugged it into his GPS.

Moments later he stopped short of his destination, not sure what to do. He couldn't knock on the front door. Not at this hour. Would a neighbor call in a complaint to the police if he tried to sneak around to the backyard? As he contemplated his next move, he noticed a vehicle pull out of the drive. He scooted down so the driver wouldn't see him and realized the vehicle belonged to Shawn. Damn him. He really was connected to this mess. Convinced now Lucinda must be inside, he started to jump out of his truck when his cell phone rang. His brother.

"What?" Jason barked in a low tone so no one would hear.

"Calm down. They've located her phones. Her regular phone went dark around the time she probably arrived home. The cell tower is the one closest to her apartment. The other phone is located in the cell tower range of the address we found for those suspected terrorists."

"Right. I'm a few houses down from there right now."

"Don't do anything," Trent cautioned. "Police have been notified. They'll be there within ten minutes."

"They just missed Shawn."

"FBI Shawn?"

"Yeah. I spotted him driving away a moment ago."

"It's okay. We'll deal with him later. The cops will rescue Lucinda. I'll let them know you're in the area, but are *doing nothing*. Got it?"

"Understood. Tell them when she comes out of the house I'll join them." He'd do anything to hold her in his arms again. Safe.

"You shouldn't do that, but I know I'd do the same if it were Shelby. I'll tell them so they don't shoot you."

He snorted. "I'd appreciate that." Knowing Trent said it in an effort to lessen the tension, he added, "I appreciate everything."

"Of course."

The moment he disconnected he saw the garage door go up. Inside stood a white Camry and a blue van. The van pulled out then the garage door lowered.

What now? Was Lucinda still inside the house or were they taking her someplace else? Making an instant decision, he started the car and followed the van. If she remained in the house the police would have her safe in a few minutes. Otherwise, they wouldn't find her at all. If they were moving her, the best way to know where they took her would be for him to follow.

After driving more than thirty minutes, the van pulled into a warehouse in the industrial area. A few cars were parked near. *What was this all about?*

CHAPTER THIRTY-THREE

Lucinda woke up with a pounding headache. Her eyes were again blindfolded. Remaining still, she took inventory of her circumstances. Bound hand and foot to two different objects. Both metal. She was prone on the floor, probably concrete considering the cold, hard surface. No zip ties this time, duct tape. The air smelled musty. The logical conclusion would be a basement. In the same house? Someplace new? She couldn't feel the phone in her back pocket. Damn. Knowing her phone could be traced, they probably moved her while she'd been out. The taste of fear filled her mouth.

"Hey, are you awake?" a female voice not far away asked.

"Yeah. Where are we?"

"No idea. How come you're blindfolded? I'm not. No gag for either of us. Of course, it doesn't matter. I've been screaming and nothing's happened. Except they dumped you in here a while ago."

"How long? Do you know how long I've been here?"

"It's not like I have a watch or anything to tell time," the girl responded in a snarky voice. "My best guess is about an hour. Do you have any idea what's happening?" The woman's tone changed to fear.

"Unfortunately, I have a good idea." And she didn't like it one bit. She remembered the comment Shawn made earlier. Her value went down when there were marks. Good lord.

"So, like, what?"

Lucinda took a deep breath. "They plan to sell us."

"What?" The woman's voice sounded more like a screech than a word. "No. That's illegal. They can't do that." Her voice rose to a high pitch becoming louder with each word.

"Calm down. Breathe," Lucinda stated in a calm and steady voice. "We need to stay calm. Think this through logically. I'd really be glad to be wrong, but I don't think so. Since I can't see you, can you describe yourself to me?" Lucinda kept trying to push the blindfold off with her shoulder. It had been tied too tight.

"I'm nineteen, blonde, blue eyes, around five feet ten inches, a hundred-twenty-five pounds."

"What's your name?"

"Bridgett Connor."

"Bridgett, I'm Lucinda Edwards. I'm a little older and taller, but we're the same type."

"What do you mean, the same type?"

"If they are selling us, then whoever is buying wants someone like us. How long have you been here?"

"A few hours, I think. Maybe longer. They grabbed me around three in the afternoon. They drugged me when they took me. It's finally wearing off, but I have one hell of a headache."

"Has someone been following you? Do you have a stalker?"

"How'd you know?" she asked sharply. "Yeah, for about a month I've thought someone's been watching me. I told my roommate, but she called me crazy."

"They've been waiting for the right time to bring you here. Can you describe this room to me?" Lucinda tried to keep the woman talking to keep her mind off their circumstances.

"It's has concrete floors. The walls are cement blocks. Two tiny windows high up. The door is metal."

"Is there any light coming in?" Lucinda concentrated on making up questions to cope with her horrible feelings. She'd heard about women who'd been kidnapped and sold. Rescue once sold was almost impossible.

"Yeah. Probably a streetlight or something like that is outside the windows. The sun's been down a while."

"Have you heard anything?"

"A lot of car doors started slamming a few minutes ago. That's when I began screaming. No one seems to hear me."

"That's not a good sign."

"What do you mean?"

"It means people are arriving. The auction will start soon." Lucinda tamped down her own urge to panic.

"You can't be serious. You're trying to scare me. No." Lucinda heard the woman shifting around. "This can't be happening. I'm in college. My parents will freak out. Hell, I'm freaking out."

Lucinda heard the panic once again gaining momentum in Bridgett's speech.

"Stop thinking like that," Lucinda snapped. "We'll figure a way out of this. Remember my name so if you make it out and I don't you'll be able to tell the authorities about me. I work at Ft. Jackson as a computer specialist. What about you?" Lucinda tried again to make the woman think of something else. It helped her as well.

"I'm a student at USC. A sophomore. I'm from Aiken."

"I used to be stationed at Ft. Gordon. I know the area."

"You're in the army?" the woman asked with surprise.

"Not any more. I was. Now I work as a civilian."

"Oh."

"I know I'm duct taped to something metal. What about you?" She needed to free herself and take stock of their situation.

"Yeah, although it's only my hands."

"Good. That's good. You can probably break free." Finally something positive to focus on.

"From duct tape?" The young woman sounded skeptical.

"Exactly. This is how you do it." Lucinda proceeded to describe how to use her body's momentum to break the tape.

After several tries Bridgett managed to do it.

"You're right, I did it." Her excitement gave Lucinda strength. "Let me help you." Bridgett took the blindfold off Lucinda then worked on her hands. Once her hands were free, she worked with Bridgett to sever the bonds on her legs.

"Good, that's the first step. Let's look around and see if there is anything we can use as a weapon."

The dark room made their search difficult. Nothing seemed to be in the space with them. Lucinda knelt on the floor and felt along the wall to see if more pipe like the one they'd taped her to could be found. Yes! Under the window. Attached to the wall, but loose. Yanking and pulling, twisting and tugging, she managed to free a twelve-inch section. Not very big around, about an inch, but heavy.

She handed it to Bridgett. "Here, take this. I might be able to work another section loose. Stand by the door. If someone comes in, hit them over the head."

"I don't know if I can do that." Bridgett sounded uncertain about her abilities.

"Remember, these people are going to sell us. What happens after we leave here won't be fun. Do it because life as you know it will be over if you don't." Lucinda spoke with a sharp, stern voice.

Changing a person's normal mindset to not do harm to another wasn't easy. She prayed the girl's will to stay free would win out. She saw the white part of the girl's eyes grow as she nodded her understanding.

Lucinda located a small section of pipe, only a few inches long. She struggled to release it then heard voices and footsteps in the hall. Damn. More than one. No way would Bridgett manage to hit more than one person. At last, Lucinda twisted off the small piece. Too small to use like the one Bridgett had. Deciding it could give extra power to her punch, she scurried over to where they'd dropped the blindfold. Lucinda wrapped the pipe in her hand to hold in place and cover her knuckles. The door opened.

Bridgett swung so hard she fell down while hitting the first person who entered the room. The other person started, which gave Lucinda the couple of extra seconds she needed to reach across both bodies and land a solid punch to the man's jaw, knocking him out. He landed outside the room.

"Quick, Bridgett, help me pull this other guy inside." They dragged the man Bridgett hit farther into the room, followed by the one Lucinda knocked out.

"Bring that piece of pipe with you. We might need it again." Lucinda searched the men's pockets. No phone. Her hands shook so hard she almost dropped the one thing worth taking. A syringe full of some liquid. More drugs for them both, no doubt.

"What do we do now?" Bridgett whispered when they were in the hallway.

Matching her whisper, Lucinda replied, "Let's find a way out. They came from the left so we'll go right. See if we can discover another exit."

"I'm scared. What if we can't?"

"Think positive. We have to. No other choice."

CHAPTER THIRTY-FOUR

Jason sat in his truck behind some dumpsters, watching and waiting. About two hours later his phone rang. Trent.

"I have bad news." Jason heard the dread in Trent's voice. "Lucinda wasn't in the house. No one there at all."

"That's what I figured." He was unhappy about the circumstances, but happy he'd followed the van.

"What do you mean?" Trent's voice perked up.

"Right after I talked to you the blue van that had been following me left the house. I tailed it. I figured if Lucinda remained in the house the cops would save her. If she was in the van, the only way we'd know where they were taking her would be for me to follow them."

"Good thinking," Trent said. "They did find her throw-away phone at the house. They'd left it on so we'd track it to the house. So where are you?"

"In the warehouse district. I didn't see any street signs. I can't figure out what's going on."

"What do you mean?" Trent asked with a cautious voice.

"The van pulled into the warehouse. A couple minutes ago a whole lot of cars started arriving. Expensive cars. Men in suits climbing out and entering through another door adjacent to the garage entrance. There are a couple men checking IDs before allowing anyone to enter. What are they doing at this time of night around here? Does it have to do with Lucinda? If not, then why is she here?"

Jason heard Trent's quick inhale. "Oh, my God. Don't panic."

Annoyed, Jason asked sharply, "What? Do you know what's happening?"

"I can guess." Once again Jason heard the dread in Trent's voice. "It's an auction."

"An auction? Here? What does that have to do with Lucinda?"

"Stay calm. Don't shout when I tell you." Over the phone Jason heard Trent's deep intake of breath. "She's the one being auctioned."

The words exploded from his mouth in a strained whisper. "No. That's not possible. How do you know? I have to get her out of there."

"Hold on. Don't do anything yet. Let me explain," Trent insisted. "We've been told about several human trafficking rings here in South Carolina. The FBI and local police are working to eliminate them. I'll call it in. You stay out of sight until help arrives. I'm on my way. I left after your first call so I'll be there soon."

Jason dropped the phone on the seat and took his weapon out of the case, rechecking it to ensure he'd chambered a round. He sat for a few minutes. His mind raced while planning and discarding ways to break into the building to rescue Lucinda.

How could this happen? He had to find Lucinda and tell her he loved her. What? Yes. He did. It took him a moment to take in the realization. They deserved to have a happy life. He'd make sure they did.

CHAPTER THIRTY-FIVE

Lucinda and Bridgett crept through the giant warehouse, leaving the sounds of people talking behind them. The dank smell of mold, dirt, and stale air hung heavy. Unable to find an exit on the ground floor they climbed the stairs one story up where they saw windows.

"Maybe we can climb out of a window then on to an adjacent rooftop," Lucinda suggested.

"I'm afraid of heights. I can't jump." Bridgett stared at her with a terrified expression.

"I don't plan to jump either. Maybe there is a fire escape ladder or something."

"Okay." Her voice sounded uncertain.

Grime kept them from seeing through the windows. Lucinda took her shirt tail and swiped off some of the filth in order to peer outside. "Not enough light to see through this gunk. I'm not sure what's out there."

"Can you open the window?" Bridgett asked.

Lucinda struggled with the rusted crank. "No. We could break it, but the noise would draw anyone searching for us right on our heels."

"We have to get out of here." Bridgett's voice rose a pitch higher. "They'll find us sooner or later."

Frantic to keep both of them calm, Lucinda strained to see an option. "Look. Over there." She pointed to the left, a few feet away. "One of the windows is broken. Maybe we can see outside."

They scrambled over debris and broken glass. Damp fresh air rushed through the opening. Then they heard feet running up the stairs.

"They've found us. Let me have that pipe for a minute. I'll break the glass and see if we can climb out." Grabbing the larger weapon from Bridgett, Lucinda broke out more glass only to discover the drop to the ground and another building was too far away to matter.

"Damn." She turned to the woman. "Run. I'll try to keep them busy while you find a way out."

Bridgett hesitated a moment then nodded and took off like her life depended on it. It did.

Lucinda did her best to provide as much time as possible for Bridgett. Obviously, the two men sent to recapture them didn't want to hurt the merchandise so they didn't use guns or knives. They kept trying to grab her hands and feet to render her helpless. She connected several times with the long pipe on their arms and torso, never able to land a significant blow to their heads. The hand-to-hand combat training she'd learned in the army helped.

One of the men succeeded in capturing her left arm then she rapped his knuckles, causing him to curse a blue streak. She heard a crunch and smiled at the thought she'd broken his hand. However, the move had given the other one an opening to lock his hand around her right wrist, forcing her to drop the large piece of pipe. She struck out with her left hand which held the small pipe and connected with his jaw. They still managed to subdue her although she continued struggling to keep them both too busy to track down Bridgett. She prayed she'd given the girl enough time to find a way out. And get help.

CHAPTER THIRTY-SIX

Jason couldn't remain in the car another moment. He climbed out of his truck after removing the bulb from the interior light so as not to give away his position. Patrolling carefully around the area, he tried to find another entrance without guards. That's when he saw her. A blonde woman. Damn, not Lucinda, her hair was too long. So who the hell was she? Someone else captured by these men? If so, she'd be scared, he realized. Not knowing him, she might scream if he approached her. What could he do?

Putting the gun behind his back, he held up both hands then walked slowly toward her. Giving her time to spot him. Once she did, he stopped.

Before she had time to run away, he said softly, "I'm not one of them. I'm looking for Lucinda. Do you know where she is?"

The question made her pause. Fear engulfed her like a blanket. "Lucinda?" She asked in a whisper while looking in every direction.

"Yes. I followed the people who brought her here. The police are on their way. Are you okay?"

Shaking, she asked, "How do I know you aren't one of them?"

"I guess you don't." Frantic to say the right thing, he said, "Tell you what. If you allow me to take the keys out of my pocket I'll toss them to you. My truck is behind some dumpsters over there." He motioned with his head. "Take it and leave. Tell me about Lucinda," he begged.

"She's inside." The young woman started crying. "We tried to escape. They found us then she attacked the two men who came after us to give me time to find a way out."

"Is she okay?" He didn't think taking on two men would end well for her.

Between sobs the woman managed to say, "I don't know. I heard a lot of fighting. I didn't look back."

"Okay. That's okay." He tried to keep his voice soft and comforting. "They probably don't want to hurt her." At least, he hoped they wouldn't. "They have other plans."

"Yeah, she told me." The girl shuddered. "When are the cops going to be here?"

"Soon. Is it okay if I give you the keys?"

"Yeah." After he tossed the keys in her direction, she asked, "What are you going to do?"

"What do you want me to do?" The last thing he needed was for her to freak out.

"Stay here until I make it to the truck."

He instantly agreed. "Of course. Where's the door you escaped from?"

"Not a door. A window on the second floor." She pointed in the direction where he'd seen her appear. "About halfway down there is a fire escape."

"Thanks." Despite his promise Jason sprinted toward the entrance seconds after the girl took off toward his truck. Nothing mattered except finding Lucinda.

After locating the fire escape ladder, he climbed up to the window as quickly and with as little noise as possible. Stopping short, he began to peer through the window to discover if any of the men were within view before climbing through. A man's hand shot out the window almost punching him in the face. He grabbed it with one hand while hanging onto the ladder with the other. He yanked down hard and the man screamed in pain.

CHAPTER THIRTY-SEVEN

The men duct taped her hands behind her then jabbed a needle in her arm.

"There, that should keep you docile," the one with the broken bones said as he shoved her toward the stairs. "Find the other girl," he snarled.

Shit, what the hell did they give me?

After they descended the stairs and walked a short distance, she heard the other man's scream.

"Damn. Now what?" Her captor pushed her again. "Keep moving."

Trying to keep her eyes open and not stumble, she moved in a fog.

"Make it snappy. We're already late."

Moments later, they arrived at a door with another guard. "It's about time you showed up. The boss is pissed you're so late. Where's the other girl and Jake?"

"Jake's rounding her up. I need a doctor."

"What? You let some skinny bitch hurt you?" The man snickered.

"Shut up." The other man growled. "You try grabbing hold of a hellcat with a lead pipe while not bruising her."

"Okay, okay. I'll have her cleaned up while you see the doc."

Grabbing Lucinda by her upper arm, the new guard shoved her through the doorway where a team of people stood waiting.

Not liking the looks of this, she asked, "What the hell are you planning to do?" Much to her dismay her words came out slurred.

"Shut up. If you don't cooperate, we'll give you another dose. Then we'll be able to do anything we like. Is that what you want?"

Not wanting to risk having more drugs administered, Lucinda stripped when instructed, took a shower, and then she was rubbed down with oil all over her body, making it gleam. She put on the gauze mini dress they handed her; covering her, but revealing more than she cared to. One person blew dry her hair while another applied make-up to the bruise left by the Korean who'd slapped her. Someone doused her with perfume. Opium. The amount so great she almost gagged.

All the information registered in her foggy brain and she knew they were prepping her for sale. Not allowing the humiliation to debilitate her took a major effort. She needed to be ready when help arrived. She needed to see Jason again. Tell him she loved him. This whole episode made her realize what's important in life. Being with someone you love. Having a family to care for.

Since Bridgett wasn't here with her, it gave her hope that help would arrive in time. Trying to think of a way to slow down the proceedings, she pretended to faint.

"What the hell?" The guard stood over her.

One of the team members said, "You must have given her too much. Find the doc."

Moments later, someone stuck smelling salts under her nose. Unable to fake her reaction, she jerked up to a sitting position.

"What happened?" She pretended to be disoriented.

"You fainted. Now stand up so we can finish this."

Unable to contrive another way to postpone the inevitable, she put on the five-inch heels they gave her and wobbled into another room with as much confidence as she could muster.

Before she could walk onto a make-shift stage, a menacing voice insisted, "Strut back and forth. Give the men a good look at you. Now!"

As instructed, she strutted onto a platform where low lights spotlighted her while the audience sat in the dark.

The room had been lavishly decorated. She noticed someone passing out drinks to the seated men. Disembodied voices discussed her attributes. The effort to stay calm and confident took a toll.

Did Bridgett manage to call for help? If so, would the police arrive in time? Had the other man tracked Bridgett down before she found a way to seek help?

A small explosion erupted. Men shouted. Booted feet ran toward her. Chaos broke out as the men in the audience took flight. Dropping to the ground, she managed to pull off one shoe. At that moment, the man who'd been behind her grabbed at her. She stabbed at his arm with the stiletto. Her effort proved weak and ineffectual. At least it slowed him down.

His cry of anger was cut short when he dropped to the floor next to her. She looked up to see Jason.

"Are you hurt?" Joining her on the floor he gathered her in his arms for a moment then he checked her over like looking for dents and scratches on his truck. "I don't see any marks. Thank God." He took off his shirt and helped her put it on, then crushed her to his chest.

Police and FBI swarmed the room, shouting as they gathered men. One stepped in front of Jason. "Hands on your head."

He did as told. "I have a gun. It's in my belt at my back. I'm Jason Meyers. Brother to Trent Meyers, Charleston PD."

The man snatched the gun then asked Lucinda, "Are you all right, ma'am?"

"Yes. This man saved me." Lucinda sounded as if marbles filled her mouth.

Jason stared at her with his eyebrows knitted together.

Keeping his gaze on Jason, the police officer said, "I'll have to check that out before we release him. Stand up." He motioned to Jason. Another officer put zip ties on the hands and feet of the man on the floor next to Lucinda.

A woman entered the room and crouched down next to Lucinda. "I'm a Victim Specialist with the FBI. I'm here to help you. Can you stand up? I brought some clothes."

"Tell them he's one of the good guys. He'd never hurt me," Lucinda insisted.

"If he is, they'll sort it out. Let me help you," the woman gently urged.

CHAPTER THIRTY-EIGHT

Only Lucinda's safety mattered to Jason. He realized she'd been drugged when he noticed her dilated eyes and heard her slurred speech. Hopefully, she'd suffered nothing worse while in the hands of those monsters. The officer zip tied Jason's hands behind his back. Herded him into a van with the scum who were responsible. He itched to do more than throw one out a window and pistol whip another. Being in a cell with them might work out okay. Trent would have him out of jail soon.

He memorized the faces in the van with him, planning to find out who the sellers and buyers were. Trent would help. Some of the men would have expensive lawyers and manage to evade jail time. He'd make it his mission to gather evidence against them. Somehow. First he'd need to take care of Lucinda.

They released Jason several hours later. Trent waited with Lucinda and Shelby as he walked out. Lucinda still wore the clothes provided by the Victim Specialist.

First, he took Lucinda in his arms. "Why aren't you in the hospital? Are you all right?" He looked into her eyes. "I mean really all right?"

"I wanted to be with you. I'm okay, thanks to you. Trent told me how you tracked me."

Jason turned to his brother. "Thanks, man. I couldn't have done this without you. I owe you big time." He put out his hand for Trent to shake.

Trent pushed it away and hugged Jason, thumping him on the back a couple of times. "We're family. You don't owe me anything."

"Come here. Let me give you a hug, too," Shelby said through her tears.

Lucinda smiled as she looked at them. Jason gathered her in his arms again. "God, I couldn't believe it when I found out you were missing. My heart almost stopped."

"Trust me. I didn't enjoy it at all." Her voice came out muffled since Jason had her crushed against his chest.

Jason asked, "So what about Bridgett? Is she okay too?"

"Yes, we spoke earlier at the hospital. I suspect she and I will both need some counseling to be completely okay. After the police took our statements, her parents picked her up."

"When you are ready to talk to someone let me know. My friend, Amy English, is a minister who can offer comfort and support. She helped me after a horrible event in my life," Shelby offered.

Lucinda nodded, but didn't speak. She walked with the group to Trent's vehicle and climbed inside.

Jason changed the subject when he saw Lucinda's eyes growing moist. "I still don't understand how all this happened. I mean, I understand the Koreans wanted Lucinda because they thought she would expose their plans. How did that morph into her being up for auction?"

"The Koreans blamed it all on Shawn. They didn't admit it, but they probably planned to kill her. I suppose Shawn figured she might have a fighting chance in this situation. He must have convinced the Koreans they could make some extra money if they sold her. He knew some of the FBI agents on the team looking into human trafficking so he probably found out some names and shared it with the Koreans. They went on the dark web and offered her up."

"Good lord, what kind of man is Shawn?" Shelby asked.

Trent went on. "Like I said, he might have thought he did her a favor by not killing her. Right now, I'm sure he's reconsidering his decision. They took him into custody at the Charleston airport about an hour ago. He had a fake passport and a ticket to Venezuela."

"No extradition," Jason stated.

"Exactly. My guess is he has some offshore account and planned to enjoy his windfall. No doubt he's been months making arrangements for all this."

Jason asked Trent, "Did the Koreans explain what they were really after?"

"No. Not yet. That could take a while and I'm sure we won't be told."

Lucinda gave Jason a funny look. "I figured it out earlier today. Or should I say yesterday?"

"What was it?"

"Sorry. I can't say. All I can say is the information has been passed on to the appropriate people. I'm sure they are handling it." She hated being so cryptic.

"Classified?" Jason asked.

She gave him a saucy grin. "I cannot either confirm or deny."

Jason blinked several times. "Wow. That serious? Never mind. I understand. I'm glad you were able to figure it out."

Arriving at Lucinda's apartment complex she led the way as they walked with her to the door.

"I don't want to be alone," Lucinda said when Jason started to unlock her door.

He noticed the terror in her eyes. He gave her arm a squeeze and smiled. "I understand. Do you want Shelby to stay with you?"

Grabbing one of Jason's hands, she confessed, "I'd rather have you."

"Of course." He smiled and opened her door.

Trent said the moment everyone had entered her apartment, "Shelby and I will head over to your place for what's left of the night, Jason. Is that okay?"

"Of course. Let me give you my apartment keys. Oh, and before you leave tomorrow could you take me back to my truck?" He snorted at that thought. "Well, actually, I'm not sure where it is. I gave Bridgett the keys and told her to take off."

"Not a problem. I have the keys. When the FBI and police sorted out what happened they gave them to me. Your truck is at the impound lot. Also, I took the liberty of sending texts to both your bosses. I'm sure they'll understand when you don't show up for work later."

"Thanks. Again. I didn't even think about that. Wait, how did you obtain their phone numbers?"

"I'm a police officer, remember? I have my sources. Glad I could fix it for you."

Lucinda put her hand on Trent's arm. "And thanks for rescuing my purse from the house where the Koreans took me. I'd have trouble unlocking my door without them.

Not to mention all the other stuff like my driver's license and credit cards."

"Enough of the thanks, already. I got it." His face turned red. "You're both happy. Glad I could expedite some of those details. It's the least I could do after what you've both been through. Try to grab some sleep." Without additional goodbyes, he took Shelby by the hand as they strolled back to his truck.

Jason turned to Lucinda. "What now? Do you want some tea or coffee? Are you hungry? Just want to sleep?"

"All of the above. Yes, I'm starving. Could you find something to cook while I take a shower? A long, hot one. Then I'd like to have some decaf tea – I don't want to make falling asleep any more difficult. Tea and food. Then sleep."

"Of course. You go ahead. I'm sure I can find something."

Lucinda couldn't wait to wash off the oil and perfume those horrible men had put on her.

Jason looked in her refrigerator and pantry, laughing at what he saw. More like what he didn't see. Not much to choose from. He managed to come up with ingredients for homemade mac-and-cheese. Realizing his own hunger, he made extra.

When Lucinda finally emerged from the shower, still red from the scalding water she'd used, he handed her a mug.

"I put some sugar in your tea. I know you don't usually do that, but you need it right now."

She nodded. "I heard somewhere it helped with shock. Thanks."

They took no time to polish off every morsel of the meal. Jason removed their plates, rinsed them then put them in the dishwasher. "Off to bed with you. I'll be fine on the couch."

She fidgeted, not looking Jason in the eye. "Would you mind sleeping with me? I mean. Not like the other night…"

"I understand. You need some comfort, not sex." Jason drew her in his arms. "Of course, whatever you want." It would be torture, but he had no intention of making her more uncomfortable. He hoped she'd want him sometime in the future.

"Thanks."

"I'll do it on one condition." He grinned at her as he held her at arm's length. "Stop saying thank you."

She joined him in a burst of laughter.

Jason took her in his arms again and looked her in the eyes. "Before anything else happens I need to tell you something," he whispered. "I love you."

A smile slowly appeared on Lucinda's face. "That's good because I love you, too."

Jason touched his lips to her. "Perfect."

EPILOGUE

Three months later, Jason stood in the kitchen in Georgetown cooking eggs and bacon. Bread waited in the toaster, ready to be submerged at the right moment. Butter and jam stood on the table.

"Are you almost ready?" he yelled.

"Just about. Go ahead and make the toast," Trent called back.

Moments later, Trent strode into the dining area wearing jeans and a t-shirt. "Thanks, man. I appreciate it."

"We all gotta eat." Jason grinned at his brother as he set their plates on the table. "You look a little nervous."

Trent took a sip of his coffee then a bite of toast. "It's not every day a man gets married. You'd be nervous too."

"Shelby and you will be totally happy together. No doubt in my mind." Jason dug into his breakfast.

"You're right. Not sure what I'm nervous about."

They ate in companionable silence, happy they'd resolved their differences months ago. He'd had no idea Trent sacrificed so much for himself and their mother. Including entering the military so he could have a steady income to help support them. Not to mention the bonuses he'd received when he volunteered to deploy to Afghanistan and Iraq as well as the combat pay. That money had paid for Jason's college. Of course, if he'd known it then, being the stupid kid he was, he would have resented Trent. Trent knew that. Jason snorted as he shook his head.

"What's so funny?" Trent stood to clear the table.

"Nothing. Well, actually thinking about what a pain-in-the-ass little brother I was a short time ago. I appreciate you hanging in there with me."

Trent gave him a mischievous grin. "I had to. Who else would be my best man at my wedding if I didn't straighten you out?"

Jason punched Trent lightly followed by Trent returning the jab. Then Trent put Jason in a mock choke hold. The doorbell rang.

"Who's that?" His voice emerged muffled due to the elbow around his throat.

Trent released Jason with a little shove toward the door. "Answer it and find out. I need to start putting on my fancy duds for the wedding. Don't forget you still have to take a shower."

Jason strode to the door and opened it to find Mr. Harper. "Come in. I didn't think we'd see you until we arrived at the church."

"Sorry to intrude. I have something you need to see." He handed a manila envelope to Jason. "Your mother asked me to deliver this at the right time."

Assuming the package must be a missive congratulating Trent on his upcoming nuptials, Jason said, "Do you want to give it to Trent? He's the one getting married."

"No, no. That's not what this is about," Mr. Harper insisted. "You read it first then share with your brother. I'm sure you'll both have questions. If you can drive to the church a little early, I'll be waiting to tell you everything I know."

"This can't wait until Trent returns from his honeymoon?"

"No, it can't. I'll explain later." Mr. Harper almost ran back to his car. Considering his eighty-plus years that took some doing.

Jason sat down at the recently cleared kitchen table and took out the contents of the mysterious package. Puzzled but not concerned, he read the first document written in his mother's own hand.

My dearest boys,

Mr. Harper will give you this letter when the time is right. I wanted to tell the both of you for years. However, I didn't want to get your hopes up, or mine. He must have been found if you are reading this note. You have another brother.

ABOUT THE AUTHOR

Rebecca Bridges worked more than thirty years for the Department of the Army as a computer specialist. A few of those years she held the title of Information Assurance Manager. In addition she served eight years as a Warrant Officer in the U.S. Army Reserves while performing the duties of security specialist for the 902 MI Group for three of those years.

Rebecca and her husband retired near the ocean in South Carolina. Her days are filled with writing, traveling and spoiling grandchildren.

For more information about Rebecca Bridges and her novels please visit her website:

http://www.RebeccaBridgesAuthor.com

www.ingramcontent.com/pod-product-compliance
Lightning Source LLC
Chambersburg PA
CBHW021319250626
47155CB00002B/545